FRESH LINEN FRAUD

CLAIRE'S CANDLES - BOOK 5

AGATHA FROST

WANT TO BE KEPT UP TO DATE WITH AGATHA FROST RELEASES? *SIGN UP THE FREE NEWSLETTER!*

www.AgathaFrost.com

You can also follow **Agatha Frost** across social media. Search 'Agatha Frost' on:

Facebook
Twitter
Goodreads
Instagram

Claire's Candles

1. Vanilla Bean Vengeance

2. Black Cherry Betrayal

3. Coconut Milk Casualty

4. Rose Petal Revenge

5. Fresh Linen Fraud (NEW!)

6. Toffee Apple Torment (PRE-ORDER!)

Peridale Cafe

1. Pancakes and Corpses

2. Lemonade and Lies

3. Doughnuts and Deception

4. Chocolate Cake and Chaos

5. Shortbread and Sorrow

6. Espresso and Evil

7. Macarons and Mayhem

8. Fruit Cake and Fear

9. Birthday Cake and Bodies

10. Gingerbread and Ghosts

Other

INTRODUCTION FROM AGATHA FROST

Hello there! Welcome to another installment of my ***Claire's Candles Cozy Mystery*** series! If this is a return visit to Northash, welcome back, and if this is your first visit, *welcome*! Since this is the fifth book in a series with overlapping subplots, I recommend staring with the first book in the series, **Vanilla Bean Vengeance**, although the mystery in this story can be enjoyed as a standalone (and I never leave a mystery hanging).

Another note: I am British, and Claire's Candles is set in the North West of England. Depending on where you live, you may come across words/phrases you don't understand, or might think are spelt wrong (we love throwing the 'u' into words like 'colour'). If that's the case, I hope you enjoy experiencing something a little different, although I believe that anyone speaking any variety of English will be able to enjoy this book, and isn't reading all about learning?

Please, enjoy! And when you're finished, don't forget to leave a review on Amazon (they help, a lot), and to check out my other series, Peridale Cafe, which has over 20 cozy adventures for you to enjoy!

CHAPTER ONE

*C*laire's mother had on her 'everything is fine' face. The perfected expression might convincingly deflect untrained eyes, but Claire had caused it enough times to recognise that clenched jaw and toothless smile that didn't quite reach the eyes. As recently as last weekend, Janet had sustained the look at a Women's Institute party for close to four hours after Claire dared to make a slightly off-colour joke.

Even after thirty-five years, the look still mildly frustrated Claire, but she'd learned to find the humour in how polar opposite she and her mother were when it came to levels of filter. Once they were alone, the look nearly always dropped with a hefty sigh and a pointed "Why did you have to say *that?*"

Claire could cope with that.

Laughing it off was easy enough.

But seeing that look when they were alone – and knowing she hadn't caused it with an ill-timed joke about Boris Johnson walking into a Berlin bar – was a different beast entirely.

Seated at her dressing table, Janet seemed to be using every ounce of her energy to keep up the smile. She stared stiffly at her reflection washed in the setting sun's golden glow. Her trembling fingers fiddled with a diamond stud that defied attachment to her left earlobe for what felt like days. When anyone else would have huffed and given up, Janet tried to keep up the act, but she couldn't control the shaking like she could the smile.

Tonight, everything was *not* fine.

Unable to watch the unrelenting struggle, Claire pushed off the edge of her parents' perfectly made bed and took the stud. The thin post slipped through its target with ease. Janet passed Claire the small silver backing, an unsure but genuine smile breaking through the heavier than usual makeup.

"Tricky little things." Janet forced a laugh as unconvincing as her patented look, handing Claire the matching stud. "Is this all too much?"

"You look lovely."

2

"I'm not used to seeing myself like this." She fluffed up her bouncy, blowed-out hair, gaze still fixed on the mirror. "Found the girl on the internet. She was the only one with pictures of people my age. Fifty pounds for hair and makeup, and she was in and out in an hour." Raising her brows, she turned from side to side, checking out her reflection in the August evening glow once the second diamond stud was in. "Are you sure my cheeks aren't too shiny? I look sweaty."

"I think that's the look these days." Claire laughed, gripping her mother's shoulders as she ducked to meet her gaze in the mirror. "You look beautiful."

"Honestly?"

"Honestly." Claire squeezed. "You don't have to be nervous."

"I'm not nervous." Janet pushed out another uncertain laugh.

Claire watched her mother's frantic fingers fumbling with an eyebrow pencil with the compulsion of someone quitting cigarettes. Janet stopped when she noticed, clenching her hands in her lap. Her right leg bounced up and down.

"Maybe I *am* nervous," Janet admitted with a sigh, relaxing into the chair. "Forty years."

"Which is why you deserve this party tonight,"

3

Claire assured her through the mirror. "Forty years working at the post office is an achievement."

"Such a long time." She pulled her skin taut at the temples. "I don't remember getting this old. I was only a girl when I started. Worked under Mrs Webster. She's dead now." She let go and her face dropped back to its natural state. "And then there was Mr Evans. He's dead now too." Frowning, she poked at the lines between her brows. "I suppose it'll be me soon."

"Where's all this come from? You've been excited about this party for months."

"I have," she said. "I *am*. I've been thinking a lot lately."

"It's not those women's magazines, is it?" Claire glanced at the neat, colourful stack on the bedside table. "I've told you to stop wasting your time with them. They only exist to make you feel bad about yourself."

"They have some *interesting* articles, I'll have you know." Janet narrowed her eyes on Claire through the mirror. "But no, it's nothing to do with them. Two weeks ago, I was in the café with your father, talking about plans for the party. The buffet, guest list, that sort of thing, and Eugene Cropper, of *all* people, decided to *dispense* his opinion – not that anyone asked for it."

"And I guarantee he was probably joking," Claire said, trying to laugh it off. "You know what Eugene is like. He's theatrical, that's all. I bet you a fiver he was just pulling your leg."

"That's what your father said."

"What did Eugene say exactly?"

"That I had to be clinically *insane* to have worked at the same place for forty *sodding* years, and yes, I'm paraphrasing." Janet turned around in her chair. "What if he's right? I'm only a few years shy of cashing my pension. I've let myself get old without ever trying anything else. What if…"

Janet's voice trailed off, her gaze going to the bedroom door as floorboards creaked on the landing. The door opened, and Grandmother Moreen walked in, a weekend bag in the crook of her arm. One sour scan of the room was all it took for the evening warmth to take on a winter chill.

"Mother." Janet immediately rose. "What are you—"

"Was that *you* I just heard wasting your breath bemoaning getting old?" Moreen's jarringly refined voice grated like nails down a chalkboard. "Are you arrogant enough to believe the facts of life need not apply to you?"

"Mother, I—"

"Don't backchat, girl." Moreen's callous stare

snapped on Claire, giving a cutting dart up and down. "I see you are very much the *same*, Claire."

Moreen never needed to say the word 'fat'; it was always expertly implied. Once an 'educator of physical education' at a private all girls' grammar school, Moreen's obsession with weight was never far from the sharp tip of her tongue. Claire had always been grateful her grandmother's retirement had spared her the horror of being one of her students – not that she'd have passed the entry exams.

"It's nice to see you, Grandmother," Claire lied, her voice as sickly sweet as she could muster. "You look well."

Moreen grumbled in her throat as though the remark were an insult. She strode across the room, her high-necked, floor-grazing black dress clinging to a body still as slender as a girl's, even at ninety. Her advancing years only made her look more like the Victorian ghoul of Claire's imagination.

"Make up a room at once," Moreen demanded, thrusting the bag into Claire's chest. "Janet, I sincerely do not know what *possessed* you to think I would stay at the bed and breakfast."

Slightly winded, Claire watched her mother's dithering lips struggle to find words. This was the nightmare scenario they'd been avoiding for years.

"B-but you always stay at the b-bed and breakfast," Janet stuttered, clinging to the back of the chair as though it was the only thing keeping her upright. "There's never been an issue before."

"That was when two *normal* sisters ran the establishment," Moreen cried, her scratchy voice rising with every word, "not some eccentric *dandy* who fancies himself a madcap inventor!"

Though an accurate description of Fergus Ferguson, Moreen's complaints were the same reasons the new owner of the B&B amused Claire. She wouldn't waste her breath informing her grandmother that one of those 'normal' sisters was now in prison for murdering two men, and the other had fled the village under a cloud of shame.

"*Claire?*" Moreen stiffened. "Must I repeat myself?"

As much as she loathed allowing her grandmother to think she had any control over her, going along to get along was always the tactic when something brought Moreen to Northash. Once safely behind her grandmother's back, Claire offered her mother a look somewhere between support and apology. Janet sank into her dressing table chair.

"You are wearing a great deal of makeup, Janet," Moreen said as Claire left. "You look sweaty. Have you been…"

Claire dumped the bag next door. The room, once Claire's childhood bedroom – and more recently, her adult bedroom while between homes for an extended period – had reverted to its previously pristine guestroom condition. Thanks to her mother's insistence that all guest bedrooms be made up to hotel standards for this exact situation, Claire merely left the room and crept downstairs.

After checking the sitting room, she found her father and her much nicer paternal grandmother, Greta, hiding in the corner of the open-plan kitchen and dining room by the drinks cabinet.

"*Crikey!*" Greta jumped, hand on her chest. "I thought you were *her*. Did you escape unscathed?"

"Just about." Claire glanced up at the ceiling as she joined them. "I feel awful for leaving Mum up there."

"You can't help her now." Alan twisted open the cap of a new bottle of whisky. "That weekend bag she had with her? Please tell me she isn't…"

"Oh, she is."

Alan's shaky hands spilled whisky around the glass before finally pouring in enough. He tossed it back with a sharp swallow, followed by a jiggle of his cheeks.

"I can't do it again," he said, immediately refilling

his glass and two others. "We've avoided this since Christmas 1997. Why's she not gone to the B&B?"

"New ownership isn't up to snuff."

"Oh, that's *typical* Mean Moreen." Greta scowled up at the ceiling, accepting her glass. "Nothing is good enough for her. You know, I might just give her a piece of my mind."

"Mother..."

"She needs it." Greta sipped the whisky. "Oh, Alan, this is awful. Have you switched to the cheap stuff?"

"Same as I always buy."

Claire took a sip. She wasn't the biggest whisky fan at the best of times, but the drink was somewhat of a family tradition, at least on the Harris side. She could usually stomach it, but she choked and let this mouthful dribble back into the glass.

"What is that?" She cleared her throat with a cough. "That's foul."

"Honestly, it's the same stuff I always get." Alan picked up the bottle and showed them the familiar label. "Must have been a dodgy batch. I'll take it back to—"

The doorbell sang out, cutting Alan off. Claire gratefully set down her glass and left the kitchen. No visitor could be as bad as the one already upstairs.

She opened the door to Eryk Kowalski, the owner

of the post office. With his pale blond hair, milky skin, and washed-out blue eyes, she'd always found him striking, though his charismatic smile was nowhere to be seen tonight.

"Is your mother home?" Eryk asked, looking around her. "I need to talk to her."

"She's upstairs with my grandmother," Claire said, opening the door fully. "I'm sure she'd be grateful for the distraction." She laughed, but Eryk didn't crack a smile. "Why don't you wait in the lounge while I fetch her?"

Eryk stepped into the sitting room, nodding curtly to Alan, who stood clutching his house cane in the kitchen doorway. Her father looked to her as though to ask, "What's he doing here?" and Claire shrugged. As she climbed the stairs, she glanced over and watched Eryk pace in front of the fireplace, his hands behind his back.

"She *is* seeing someone," she heard her mother say in a forced hushed tone once she was in the hallway. "Do you remember Paula, who used to live next door? Her son, Ryan. They were close as children."

"That ginger lump of a lad?" Moreen replied. "That makes sense. I always told you to be stricter with Claire. I cannot believe you let her get to that size. No wonder she isn't married. At her age that is frankly—"

Claire cleared her throat; unfortunately, it was a conversation she'd heard countless times. She tried not to let the words fester, but she'd be lying if she denied the sting of her grandmother's assessments, especially since she was as happy right now as she'd ever been.

"Mr Kowalski is downstairs." Claire only looked at her mother. "He wants to talk to you."

Janet surprised Claire by not immediately grabbing the opportunity to escape with both hands and rushing out of the room. She hesitated by the dressing table before leaving, no shred of relief on her face.

"*Kowalski?*" Moreen barked, her bony fingers clutching the gold bedpost as she rose from the mattress. "What sort of name is that?"

"He's Polish."

"*Polish?*"

"Polish," Claire repeated. "As in, from Poland?"

"Don't backchat, girl."

Already knowing where the conversation was likely to go, Claire fled the instant Moreen turned to check her bound-up hair in the mirror. Her grandmother's white hair reached the bottom of her back, though Claire seldom saw it out of the uniform bun at the nape of Moreen's neck.

As she snuck back downstairs, she saw Eryk's back as he pulled the door closed behind him. She ducked in time to see her mother clutching the mantlepiece in the sitting room, her head lowered. A split second later, Janet shook out her blow-dried hair in the mirror, and the 'everything is fine' smile switched on again at full force.

"What was that about?" Claire leaned against the doorframe. "I'm guessing he didn't suddenly offer to pay for the party?"

"Nothing." Janet replied quickly, her breathing unsteady behind the smile. "Go home and get changed. The party starts in twenty minutes, and we can't be late."

Claire looked down at her hip-hugging black cigarette trousers and maroon blouse with a slight peplum flare, wondering what was wrong with them. She'd had her friend, Sally, help her pick out the outfit, precisely to avoid having the inevitable quarrel about her fashion choices today of all days.

"This is what I'm wearing."

"Fine." Janet pinched the bridge of her nose. "It'll do, I suppose."

"Mum?" Claire asked softly. "Are you okay? What did Eryk—"

"I'm fine, Claire!" Janet cried, manic eyes at odds with the fake smile. "I'm *fine.*"

"*Janet?*" Moreen thundered from upstairs. "These bed sheets simply will not do."

Janet exhaled and mounted the bottom step, though she didn't make it any further. As she clutched the bannister, her smile vanished and mascara-tinged tears left tracks on her shiny cheeks.

"Mum?"

"Cancel the party," she said in a low voice, pulling out her diamond studs and letting them drop onto the carpet.

"*Janet?*" Alan hobbled down the hallway with his cane, Greta behind him. "What's happened? What did Eryk—"

"*Cancel the party!*" she cried, glaring at them through a mask of ruined makeup. "Cancel it. Cancel it *right now!*"

Leaving her earrings behind, Janet hurried upstairs. The master bedroom door slammed, and the key twisted in the lock.

"What was that about?" Greta whispered. "She's been sending out invitations for this party for weeks. Half the village will be there."

"I'll call The Hesketh Arms," Alan said with a sigh, already limping to the hallway phone. "I think it's best we give her some space."

While her father lied on the phone about food

poisoning, and Moreen's demands went unanswered, Claire plucked the diamond studs from the carpet. She'd never seen her mother's 'everything is fine' veneer so completely shatter – not even after her own father's death.

What had Eryk said?

And why tonight of all nights?

CHAPTER TWO

ears of working on the Warton Candle Factory's production line had turned Claire into a natural early riser. Weekday or weekend, her eyes usually sprang open at seven on the dot.

One year ago, she'd have awoken in her parents' house with a groan. Mornings started with a half-asleep shower, followed by her mother's constant wittering over a slice of toast. After her last gulp of cold coffee, she'd bomb up steep Warton Lane, rain or shine. At least three times a week, she barely made it on time. Every so often, she had waded through the field behind her house as a muddy shortcut, much to Ian Baron's fist-shaking anger.

Claire's mad morning rush, her mother called it.

When the rushes were the maddest, they could sour Claire's day before it had a chance to get going.

She hated mornings.

At least, she used to.

Unless she'd had one too many pints after work with Damon the night before, most mornings started with a smile these days. Waking up with her two cats, Sid and Domino, in her cosy flat, conveniently positioned above her candle shop, had that effect on her. Seventeen years grinding away as an anonymous cog at the factory had made Claire forget how pleasant mornings could be.

These days, she took pleasure in the quiet hours before the square came to life, especially now they were in the middle of summer. Most mornings, she'd go down to the shop with the cats an hour before opening to prepare for the day. In between sips of hot coffee, she'd straighten every label while singing badly to throwback songs on Heart Radio.

No candle factory.

No mad rush.

No comments from her mother.

What better way to start a day?

But on this Saturday, Claire awoke full of dread for the first time in recent memory. Even though there was no mad rush to be had, she couldn't manage a smile. Thoughts of her mother consumed her.

Claire dragged herself out of bed, and after the cats were fed, the three of them trundled downstairs. Lit by the dust-illuminating morning glow through the windows, Claire worked on her new candle formula in the shop's back room. Sid curled up in a warm spot, and Domino busied herself with the important business of knocking packing peanuts off the counter.

Claire had been dithering about the next star candle, but now she knew what it had to be.

Fresh linen.

Her mother's favourite.

A refreshing powdery scent with the right balance of floral and citrus notes would be a great seller. She had a basic fresh linen scent she'd developed before first opening, but she wanted these to have the best fresh linen scent ever to greet a nostril.

"Someone's been busy this morning!" Damon announced after letting himself in and flicking on the overhead light. "Bonkers experiments?"

"You know me." Claire dropped another pipette of lemon citrus into the mix before offering it to Damon. "What's this smell like?"

"Like my mum's washed my clothes."

"Then I'm getting there." She added another drop of

white musk. "Just need to get it to where it smells like *my* mum washed my clothes."

"How's she doing? Half the village was at the pub when Malcolm announced she had food poisoning."

After finally giving up and leaving her parents' house when her mother wouldn't open the bedroom door, Claire had seen the busy pub across the square first-hand. She'd almost gone in to show her face on Janet's behalf, but unlike her mother, she'd never mastered her 'everything is fine' smile.

"It's not food poisoning."

"Oh, good." Damon reached into a bag and pulled out two dustpan-lid-sized breakfast sandwiches. "Do you want egg and bacon or bacon and egg?"

"You spoil me with choices."

Claire didn't miss working at the factory, but in those first few months that she'd run the shop alone, she had missed her partner in crime. For fifteen of her seventeen years, she'd worked alongside Damon on the production line. Thankfully, Damon bit off her hand when she offered him a job at the shop. Two weeks of having Damon by her side again, and there was nothing left to miss at the factory.

"If it's not food poisoning," Damon muttered through a ketchup-soaked mouthful, "what could have possibly made your mother pull out at the last minute? She's talked about nothing else lately."

"I wish I knew," she replied, walking over to her beloved bean-grinding coffee machine. "Eryk turned up when she was getting ready and said something."

"What?"

"No idea, but it made her snap. Told us to cancel the party and locked herself in her bedroom. She even ignored Grandmother Moreen. I thought she was going to have a heart attack from the shock of my mother not bowing to her every demand."

"Another visit from Mean Moreen already?" He shuddered. "She scares me."

"I think she means to." Claire put the first cup in place after the machine finished its rinse cycle. "What could your boss say to you that's *so* terrible you cancel your fortieth anniversary party?"

"You're my boss, and we're nearer our fortnight anniversary than fortieth, but I suppose one thing comes to mind." He dabbed the ketchup from the corners of his lips. "I've never been fired, but how did you feel when Graham gave you the sack from the factory?"

"If I'd had a party planned, I would have cancelled it," she said. "I don't think I would have taken the plunge to open this place if it hadn't happened, so it worked out for the best in the end, but it was devastating at the time."

"There's an easy way to tell." He jerked his chin in the direction of the left wall. "Post office should be open by now. Your mum has worked there every Saturday since before either of us were born. She's not the type to pull a sickie."

"That's a good idea."

"You haven't just hired me for my looks." He winked as he pushed up his glasses. "Go and have a look while I get this place opened up."

Claire handed the finished coffee to Damon and added a second cup. She hit the double espresso button before grabbing her light blue denim jacket off the wall.

Given Saturday's early close and it being the last chance to use the post office before Monday, Claire was aware how busy it would be, so she left through the back door.

In the cobbled alley behind her shop's row, the warm sun prickled her skin, promising another busy day at Claire's Candles.

She pushed on the rickety blue back gate that led into the yard behind the post office at the end of the row, two doors down. Usually it swung in, but today, it didn't budge. Had someone finally fixed the broken lock her mother had been complaining about for months? She gave it another push, and it opened half an inch. The lock was still rotted out.

She peered through the gap and gave the door another shove. Plastic bags rustled in a tall black wheelie bin. Her mother never would have blocked the exit like that unless she wanted to keep Claire out. Then again, she wouldn't have known Claire would come through the back.

Through the gap, the shadows shifted.

"Mum, if that's you, it's Claire," she called through the wood. "Leo? Mr Kowalski?"

Doubting if she'd seen anything at all, she stepped back. She wasn't about to ram the gate down to check, and she certainly wasn't going to scale the wall.

Taking the shortcut around the side of the post office, she pulled out her phone and called one of her most-used contacts.

"Hello?" said Claire's father on the other end.

"It's me," she said. "How's Mum? Is she talking yet?"

"Sort of," he whispered back. "I didn't see her all night. I kipped in the second guest bedroom. Woke up just in time to see her go out this morning."

"So, she *has* come to work?"

"I don't think so," he said. "She told me she was going for a walk. Tried going with her, but I couldn't get my shoes on quick enough. It didn't even look like she'd brushed her hair, and she left without opening the curtains or making the bed. Any other time and I'd say it was refreshing, but you know what your mother is like. I'm worried about her."

"Me too," Claire replied. "How long has she been out?"

"An hour?" he suggested. "Do you think I should go looking for her? I thought she'd be back by now."

"She'll come back," Claire said, looking around the small crowd gathered in front of the post office for any sight of her mother. "Do you think there's a chance she's been fired?"

"I didn't want to say it, but what else could it be? I'd better go, little one," he whispered over the sound of Moreen screaming for him in the background. "Your grandmother has me waiting on her hand and foot, and she doesn't seem rushed to catch her train home."

Claire hung up and approached the dozen or so people waiting outside the post office. The square was growing busy as shops, including Claire's Candles, opened for the day. Still, the concentration outside the post office wasn't average, even for a Saturday.

"Get in line, love," an old woman called to Claire, hooking her thumb down the back. "Some of us have been waiting for ages."

"It should be open," she said, almost to herself.

"Well, it's not," another woman barked. "Back of the line. I've got a cheque to cash in."

Claire gave the door a single shove to confirm it was locked. The large bay windows were hidden entirely behind vinyl, and the sea of posters in the door window obscured the view inside. Like in the yard, she thought she saw movement but didn't dare linger in case the mob turned on her.

"Not open," Claire said as she walked into her shop. "Oh, hi, Ryan."

Ryan turned around, the hazy morning sun lighting up his freckles and red hair. Like most days, he was in his gym clothes.

"Morning, Claire," he said, lifting a large bouquet of orange and yellow flowers off the counter. "You look nice."

Despite what was going on, the mere sight of Ryan brought a smile to Claire's face. Friends since childhood, they were a month into their 'let's see how things go' romantic trial.

"One for you," he said, pulling apart two normal-sized bouquets, "and one for your mother. Tell her Amelia spent ages picking them out. We're all sending our best. Hope the food poisoning isn't too bad."

"They're beautiful." Claire accepted the bouquet

and a kiss on the cheek. "You scared of my mother, Ryan?"

"It's not food poisoning," Damon said as he walked in with a box of vanilla candle jars. "Drama."

"A little," Ryan answered Claire, following Damon with his eyes. "And it's not? That's what Malcolm said at the pub."

"To cut a short story even shorter, she's upset, and I don't know why. And to make it worse, my grandmother is in town."

"Mean Moreen?" Ryan's brows shot up. "She's *still* alive?"

"No, but we thought it would be nice to dig her up for the party." Claire slapped him with the flowers. "Of course she's alive. That much venom coursing through her veins has practically pickled her. She'll be here with Cher and the cockroaches, you watch."

"Is she just as bad?"

"Oh, no." Claire shook her head. "She's worse."

"Remember that time she caught us scoffing crisps in your dad's shed," Ryan asked, his freckled cheeks tingeing red, "and made us do laps of the garden?"

"Was that the time *I* threw up or *you* threw up?" she asked, laughing more than she'd done at the time. "We went upstairs and finished our crisps both times."

"Your grandmother is crackers," Damon said, stocking the shelves.

"No, she's an *educator of physical education*," she mimicked her best Mean Moreen voice. "How *dare* any of you be *fat* in *my* presence!"

"Not so much him these days." Damon nodded at Ryan.

"I've gained a few pounds actually," he replied, patting his washboard stomach over his tight gym vest. "Had chippy twice this week."

"I had chippy twice *yesterday*." Damon fiddled with his glasses. "But keep it up, Ryan, and you might get your body fat percentage up to around three percent before the end of the—"

An air-cracking bang cut Damon off. The echo shuddered through the square, and everyone outside came to a silent halt.

"Was that a car backing up?" asked Ryan, walking over to the window.

"Sounded more like a firework." Damon pushed himself up off his knees. "Which direction did that come from? Can't make heads or tails of it."

"Those bloody kids," said Claire. "They've been letting them off in the back alley at all hours."

She marched through the back door for the second time and ripped open her yard's gate, ready to give the teenagers a piece of her mind. They always ran off before she had the chance, and she wouldn't miss her opportunity today.

She popped her head into the alley: no kids and no fireworks. The owner of the greengrocers on one side of her and the chippy on the other were doing the same. They all nodded to each other before pulling back.

"No fireworks," she said as she returned to the store.

"Why doesn't this feel right?" Damon whispered. "It's so quiet out there."

Claire joined them at the window behind her latest display of summer scents. The whisperers seemed hesitant to resume their early morning shopping as worried eyes scanned the square.

A woman's shrill scream sliced through the silence. The post office crowd fluttered away from the door like ripples after a dropped stone in a pond. Chaos took over the nothingness, and the square returned to animation as if someone had hit play after an extended pause.

Claire rested the bouquets of flowers on the basket of cherry wax melts and followed the chaos outside. The crowd ebbed and flowed around a single source, and for the third time that morning, Claire spotted movement through the gaps in the bystanders.

On the pavement outside the post office, Eryk Kowalski dropped to his knees. Even with both hands clutching his stomach, blood poured from his midsection like jam through a strainer.

Silence fell again as Eryk doubled back on himself, his hands slipping away from the wound.

"We've been burgled!" cried Leo, stumbling through the door sporting a shiny black eye. "They shot him."

"*Dad!*" a young man cried, pushing past Leo. "Someone do something!"

Claire stepped back into Ryan's arms as phones appeared from pockets. The man who reached the operator and asked for an ambulance – though it was clearly too late for that – was the first person to speak.

A question burned through Claire's mind, rinsing and repeating until she couldn't stand it. Turning, she buried her face in Ryan's chest, and he wrapped her in a tight embrace.

On any other Saturday, would that have been her mother?

CHAPTER THREE

*N*orthash had two village pubs. The Hesketh Arms, with its locally famous homebrew, was a popular meeting point in the heart of the square.

And then there was The Park Inn.

The *other* pub.

Chain run, with new faces behind the bar every other week, The Park Inn couldn't compete with the inviting, homey atmosphere Malcolm and Theresa fostered at The Hesketh. The Inn's décor was technically nicer, but its ever-updating 'local pub' aesthetic felt like it had been cooked up in a boardroom. Visitors to Starfall Park gave it enough passing trade to keep the pumps in action, but most locals shied away … unless they needed a pint with a side of privacy.

As she carried two pale pints across the pub, Claire could barely believe it was a Saturday night. The Park Inn was only moderately busy. Even with Eryk's shooting that morning – or perhaps in part because of it – The Hesketh Arms had been bursting on her way to meet her father.

On any other night, Claire would have braved the crowds and hovered for the golden opportunity to snag a seat. But tonight, The Inn was the perfect place for a pint with her dad. Though only a stone's throw from The Hesketh, Claire didn't recognise a single patron.

"Should I see if I can get a doctor to have a look at her?" asked Alan, continuing their brief conversation from outside the pub. "What if it's a nervous breakdown? I've never seen her like this."

"Knowing Mum, I'd say that'd only make things worse." Claire sipped her pint. It wasn't Hesketh Homebrew, but at least it was cold this time. "Has she mentioned why she cancelled the party?"

"No, but when I asked if she'd been fired, she locked herself in the downstairs bathroom." He sighed as he scanned the over-designed food menu. "And your grandmother being there isn't helping matters. I keep dropping hints about driving her to the train station, but she's not taking me on. It's almost like she thinks she's staying. She's been sitting in *my* armchair all day, barking orders at me like I'm not the one limping around on a cane."

Claire's gratitude for her privacy continued to swell. She'd take her chances with an armed burglar on the loose if it meant she could avoid sleeping under the same roof as her grandmother.

"How did Mum react when she heard about Eryk's shooting?"

"Like I'd told her about the weather," he said. "No reaction. And then she started scrubbing the skirting boards. She was still at it when I left. Couldn't tear her away. She's in one of her cleaning trances."

"Not the oddest thing she's done."

"I know she's not always the *warmest* woman, but she was so … *cold*. I just don't know what to…"

Alan's voice trailed off. Inhaling deeply, a polite smile transformed his expression as he looked over Claire's shoulder.

"I thought I heard your voice, Alan!" called Detective Inspector Harry Ramsbottom. "You don't mind if I join, do you? Prefer the quiet you get here, but it's always better to eat in company."

DI Ramsbottom, once a colleague of Alan's at the

local police station, dropped into the free seat with a full plate. Without waiting for their invitation, he pulled his chair close. Their pints sloshed as his belly collided with the table, spilling some of the precious contents.

"Terrible business," announced Ramsbottom as he cut into an anaemic-looking pie swimming in watery gravy. "Terrible, *terrible* business. An armed burglary right here in Northash? As if we haven't enough to contend with, some madman needs to throw a gun in the mix? Your Janet had a lucky escape with that food poisoning."

"I suppose she did," Alan replied, his politeness giving nothing away. "She's processing the news in her unique way. Any leads on the case, Detective Inspector?"

"If only." Ramsbottom spooned garden peas into his already full mouth. "My officers are out looking for anyone who matches the description Tomek gave."

"Tomek?" Claire asked.

"Eryk Kowalski's son," he revealed. "Young lad. Twenty. Apparently, he was learning the ropes with his dad at the post office when the masked burglar came in with their gun. Locked the doors and stuck 'em up like an ol' Western film. Emptied the tills. When Eryk fought back, he shot him right in the front." He patted down his pockets for his pad. "Caucasian male around five eight give or take a couple of inches, average build. Had on a balaclava and an accent that may or may not be local. They're guessing he was in his thirties, but they couldn't be too sure."

"That could be anyone," said Claire.

"I'd have a better chance finding Wally." Ramsbottom chuckled, flicking to the next page. "Saying that, it's never easy to find them after these kinds of burglaries. They usually strike at random."

"Not always," Alan pointed out.

"Still as sharp as ever," said Ramsbottom with a wag of his finger. "Whoever they were, they slipped in and out, without leaving any crumbs. Almost expert."

"Or an inside job?" Alan suggested. "How's Leo doing?"

"Of course. You'll know him through Janet." Ramsbottom flicked a few pages along. "Poor lad was shaken up. Didn't have much to say for himself. He'd just started his shift when the assailant barged in. Same story as the Kowalski boy. Screaming and shouting as they emptied the tills, Eryk gets involved, gunshot, and then our balaclava-clad friend ran out the back and down the alley."

"The back alley?" Claire's ears pricked up. "As soon as Eryk was shot?"

"That's what it's looking like."

"I tried the post office's back gate about five minutes before the shooting," Claire remembered aloud, frowning into her beer. "The bin was blocking it from the inside. I thought I saw someone, but they didn't respond when I spoke."

"Maybe *that* was the burglar?" Ramsbottom suggested as he slopped gravy down his pink tie without noticing. "Staking the place out?"

"It can't have been," she said, her frown deepening. "I walked around the front. That's when I called you, Dad."

"That was just after eight," he said. "They were still doing the top of the hour headlines on BBC Breakfast."

"And the front door was already locked," she said, her fingers fumbling with a beer mat as her mind worked, "and like I said, that was before anyone was shot, so the burglar was already in there. What time was the shooting?"

"We're estimating ten minutes past the hour."

"Quite a few people had gathered outside, so it's safe to assume the burglar was in there for what? Fifteen minutes?"

Ramsbottom stared at his notes, scratching at his unnaturally thick golden toupee with the end of his fork.

"It would seem that way," he said, stabbing four chips onto his fork and cramming them in his mouth. "It's not uncommon for some burglaries to last that long. There'll often be negotiations. There's an average time, but I can't quite—"

"Anywhere between ninety seconds and twelve minutes." Alan rattled off the fact without missing a beat. "The average is eight minutes, but having seen similar cases over the years, the business hold-ups are usually on the shorter side."

"Frenzied dash to get in and out," Ramsbottom agreed before patting down his pockets and pulling out a pen. "This is why we miss your brain at the station, Alan. You always have that extra little nugget."

Alan smiled, though Claire saw the pain behind the politeness. If he'd had his way, Alan would have never stepped down from his role as Northash's detective inspector. The brain tumour that had caused his limp and spontaneous lapses in memory hadn't forced him out, but the offer of a demotion to a dcsk job had. He missed it more than he'd ever admit.

"Might be worth double checking the alley detail too," Claire pointed out, reading Ramsbottom's scruffy handwriting upside down as he scribbled away. "I was out there not thirty seconds after the shot, thinking it was kids with fireworks. Maybe they were quick, but I didn't see anyone."

"You're sure it was the same time?"

"The greengrocers and chippy were there too if you need to crosscheck," she said. "The officer who took my witness statement didn't seem to think anything of it."

"Hmm." Ramsbottom continued to scribble. "I'll have some details clarified. The poor lads were in shock. Understandable, given the circumstances. You could forgive them for not getting the details right when it's so fresh—"

A vibrating came from somewhere on Ramsbottom's person. He dropped the pen in the gravy, tutted, and patted himself down before squeezing his phone from his trouser pocket.

"It's my lucky day," he said with a grin, hanging up after a brief phone call. "Gun's been found in the forest on the other side of the canal. Hopefully, the thing is smothered in prints so we can wrap this up quickly."

"That would make for a neat case," Alan said. "I hope that's your outcome, for all of our sakes."

"Fingers crossed." Ramsbottom plucked the rest of the pie out of the gravy pool and finished it in one bite. "Send my love to Janet."

DI Ramsbottom vanished as quickly as he'd arrived,

leaving behind his pen and plate. Though Claire hadn't wanted his company when she'd heard his voice across the pub, she was glad he'd joined them after all. She plucked a chip from his leftovers and let the details stew.

"Do you think Tomek or Leo is lying about what happened?" Alan asked, joining her in stealing a soggy chip.

"You know when you're at a party and you overhear someone telling a story about something for which you were actually present, and all you can think is that it didn't happen at all like their retelling?"

"I'm married to your mother, so yes."

"I wasn't *in* the post office," she said, picking up another chip, "and I'm not saying they're lying, but I was outside when the doors were locked, and so were tons of other people. Everyone was under the impression the post office wasn't open. Simple as that. If there was screaming and shouting happening inside, those walls must be insulated because I was right there and didn't hear a peep. Surely someone would have noticed *something* before a gunshot?"

"That's an excellent observation, little one," he said with a smile. "Let's hope Ramsbottom finds those winning prints. I'd hate to think that person is still out there, especially when they've hit so close to your shop."

They continued talking about the shop until they had drained their pints. When a rowdy group of young men bounced in wearing short-sleeved shirts and swimming in aftershave, they gave each other a nod and made for the exit.

"Thanks for meeting me, little one." Alan pulled on his jacket as they walked away from the pub. "I should probably get back to the cul-de-sac. If your mother cleans the skirting boards any longer, she'll scrub her way through the gloss. That, or she'll finally snap and murder your lovely grandmother."

"I don't think that's happening tonight," she said as they rounded the post office corner. "What are they doing there?"

Grandmother Moreen's all-black ensemble stuck out like a sore thumb in the sea of exposed sun-kissed arms and legs in the front beer garden of The Hesketh Arms.

"Oh, she's seen us," Alan whispered, waving across the square as Janet overtook her mother and opened the gate. "Are we in trouble?"

"Can't tell," she whispered back, waving. "Has Mum perked up or is she putting on *The Show*?"

"She's too far away to ... oh, no, she's furious."

"*There* you two are!" Janet cried as she crossed the square. "I thought you said you were going to meet Claire at the pub?"

"The *other* pub."

"Why would you go to the *other* pub?"

"My fault," Claire lied as her creative juices kicked in. "I … erm … got a little too drunk last time I was in there and got a bit carried away on the karaoke machine. Didn't want to face Malcolm and Theresa until they'd had time to forget."

Janet grumbled as her narrowed gaze flitted between them. Her gaze darted to the post office, but as though nothing remarkable had ever happened there, she turned away and waited for her mother to catch up.

Claire looked at the spot where Eryk had succumbed to his wound. The smooth paving stone was scoured of blood, but she could still see him lying there.

"Mother insisted we eat out," Janet explained dryly when Moreen mounted the kerb.

"I came here on the promise of a party and you have kept me cooped in your house every passing second since." Moreen glared around the square with a puckered nose. "What's that smell?"

"I think that's the chippy," said Claire.

"You mean the fish and chip shop," Moreen corrected. "Janet, since you took me to a *dump* of a pub and then promptly dragged me out again, I insist we dine at the fish and chip shop. I am famished and cannot handle being hauled across the village to yet another hovel."

"There's no indoor dining," said Janet.

"Oh, for goodness' sake!" Moreen cried, clasping her hands tightly at her middle. "And you wonder why I moved away so long ago. Where else might we eat?"

"Marley's could still be open," Alan suggested. "It's a vegan café just around the—"

"What possessed you to think I would eat *vegan* food?" Moreen snapped, her eyes going to the summery display in the candle shop window. "I assume *this* is the shop you were telling me about, Janet? Unless there's *another* Claire in the village who would open an entire shop devoted to something as frivolous as candles?"

"It's my shop, Grandmother."

"Then we shall take the fish and chips wrapped and eat in your flat."

"What?" Claire's heart sank.

"Are you suddenly afflicted with deafness?" Moreen asked with pursed lips. "Don't backchat, girl."

"Why can't we take it back to the cul-de-sac?"

"Because your grandmother wanted a change of scenery," Janet hissed, gripping the back of Claire's arm as though to say, 'play along, or else'. "Why don't you get the *tea* ready while we order the food?"

Janet didn't stick around for Claire to argue. Alan apologised with his eyes but followed them into the chippy.

Claire knew what her mother had really meant by 'get the tea ready'. Janet had inherited her cleaning habits directly from her mother. If most things weren't clean enough for Janet, *nothing* was ever clean enough for Moreen. Claire kept her flat tidy by most people's standards, but any level of 'lived in' might as well have been a rubbish dump in their eyes.

While the kettle boiled, Claire rushed from one end of the flat to the other, scooping up anything and everything in sight. Pyjama bottoms left in the kitchen, a bra strewn over the sofa, a jacket hooked on a chair. The DVD cases flew under the TV stand and she bashed the cushions together for a quick fluffing. There was no way to disguise the overflowing washing basket in her bathroom, so into the bath it went, with fervent hopes Grandmother Moreen didn't pull back the shower curtain and insist on a bubble bath.

By the time the door to her shop opened downstairs, she'd whizzed around the flat half a dozen times, lit every candle in sight, and made it back to the kitchen in time for the kettle to ping.

"Unbelievable, Claire," Janet whispered as she rushed into the flat with their food. "You could have tidied up!"

Moreen followed, hands clasped, nose wrinkled, and eyes scanning. Always scanning, like the Terminator on his search for Sarah Connor. Except instead of humanity's last hope, she was looking for dust and clutter. Despite her insistence on eating at Claire's, anyone seeing her expression would have thought the mysterious gunman had forced her in.

"Small," she concluded as she crept in, still inspecting. "Everything is in a *single* room."

"Except the bathroom and bedrooms," Claire replied with the biggest smile she could muster. "Cosy, don't you think?"

"If you like."

Usually, Claire would eat her chippy supper straight from the paper in front of the telly. After all, that's how it was meant to be eaten to avoid washing unnecessary plates.

Moreen asserted they dine at the small circular table crammed behind the sofa at the back of the flat. With only two chairs, which went to Moreen and Janet, Claire perched on a small footstool taken from her bedroom and her father sat on an upturned mop bucket topped with a pillow.

While they ate, Moreen complained about everything and anything in a never-ending stream. The food, the flat, the weather, the village, her present company. The lack of silences to fill meant Claire could tune out. She kept her eyes on her mother, who was clearly back to putting on her best act despite the morning's horror.

When the incessant stream of complaints dried up, Janet stacked their plates and carried them through to the kitchen. After showing her grandmother to the bathroom, Claire joined her mother at the kitchen sink, sensing her moment.

"If you're about to ask how I am," Janet said as she scraped Moreen's picked over leftovers into the bin, "I'm absolutely—"

"*Fine?*"

"As it happens, yes."

"And the fact that your boss was shot this morning?" Claire whispered, glancing back at the table. Alan sleepily watched the sunset through the small window directly in line with the clocktower in the square. "You saw him the night before he was killed."

"What are you doing, Claire?" Janet twisted on the taps. "Are you trying to *upset* me?"

"Quite the opposite." Claire rested a hand on her mother's shoulder; Janet promptly shrugged it off. "I'm trying to figure out what has hurt you so much that you feel you need to put on a charade."

"I'm *fine*."

"You're *not*." Claire reached across her mother and squirted washing up liquid into the filling sink. "Mum … did Eryk fire you last night?"

"Don't be silly." She forced a breathy laugh between each word, not missing a beat. "Honestly, Claire! *Yes*, it's a shame what happened to Eryk, but I won't pretend like I enjoyed the man's company just because he's dead. Maybe now the post office will have some *real* leadership. That man's been cutting corners all year to save a few pounds here and there. Knock-off alcohol and dodgy cigarettes from abroad, and food barely grazing the sell-buy dates. It's been embarrassing. He's been a dreadful boss."

"But what did Eryk *say* to you last night?"

"Do I have to tell you everything?" Janet dunked the first plate into the water and scrubbed like her life depended on it. "It was a simple misunderstanding, okay?"

"You cancelled your party."

"I wasn't feeling well."

"You know you don't *actually* have food poisoning, right?"

"Claire, *drop it*." Janet passed the plate for Claire to dry. "Why don't you go—"

"*Appalling!*" Moreen exclaimed as she walked back in. "Claire, you should be ashamed of yourself. Do your laundry, girl."

"Why don't I what?" Claire asked, ignoring her grandmother.

"Find some dessert from somewhere?" Janet pulled her handbag off the counter and thrust a ten-pound note at Claire. "You know how your—"

"*Janet?*" Moreen cried as she returned to the table and sat primly. "Will there be a sweet after such an incredibly salty course?"

Glad to escape her invaded flat, Claire left without discussion. Knowing nowhere would be open to get dessert quickly and not wanting to chance her grandmother's vegan baking detection skills, Claire walked around the corner. Positioned in a short row of shops at the foot of steep Park Lane, the all-hours supermarket had become a dangerous place for Claire. No matter the time, no matter the craving, it was only ever a minute's walk away.

Scanning the limited selection of dessert options in

the shop's fridges, she heard 'Janet' on the next aisle over. Pulling away from the fridges, she leaned into the rows of chocolate bars, hearing her mother's name again.

"That's what Karen said she *saw*," a woman whispered. "A blazing row with Janet at the post office and now he's *dead*!"

"Funnily timed food poisoning then, don't you think, Joan?" someone replied. "Saying that, Bridget texted me saying she *just* saw Janet at the pub. Looked like she's had a swift recovery."

"You think she'd fake food poisoning to get out of the party?"

"That, or to give her an alibi that keeps her out of the picture," she whispered back. "You *know* what Janet is like. She can't take people talking to her the way she talks to everyone else. I'll put money on her having set this whole shooting up to get her own back on that poor man."

"Oh, Linda, you are naughty!"

"It's only what all the girls are saying."

The voices moved away, and Claire resumed scanning the aisles, though she couldn't focus on the labels. The two women rounded the corner, and their whispering stopped when they spotted Claire. She didn't know either of them personally, but she'd seen them enough times at her mother's Women's Institute functions to know they were part of her mother's stuffy circle.

"You should be careful what you say when you think no one is listening," Claire muttered as they sauntered past. "Narrow aisles."

Leaving the slack-jawed women to scramble for their comebacks, she picked out three boxes of cream cakes and took them to the self-checkout. On her way out of the shop, she gave Linda and Joan another glance, but they were deep in their whispering again as they examined bottles of wine.

Back at her flat, she was surprised, though relieved, to see her mother pulling up in her car. Moreen strode through the front door and climbed into the passenger seat, ignoring Claire like she wasn't there – just how Claire preferred it.

"Your grandmother is having one of her migraines," Alan explained. "Claims all your lit candles caused it."

"Do you think I should start advertising their mean-grandmother-repelling properties?" Claire glanced into the car as her mother checked her reflection in the pull-down mirror. To her father, she whispered, "Listen, did Mum get back from her walk *before* or *after* Eryk was shot?"

"After," he replied. "Little one, I don't think your

mother—"

"Neither do I," she interjected, "but I just overheard two of her WI pals in the shop. Apparently, Karen overhead Mum and Eryk arguing at the post office. Let's just say the gossips' imaginations are already running wild."

He sighed. "As I feared."

"You know Mum won't be able to handle that right now," she said, gulping, "no matter how wide she pushes that smile."

"Are you suggesting we try to clear her name before the rumours stick?"

"I think I am."

"Then I'll try to get some answers out of her." He leaned in and kissed Claire on the cheek. "Let's hope she doesn't lock herself away again."

After waving them off, Claire went up to her flat and slumped in the middle of the sofa. She flicked on the telly and scanned the various films and TV shows on offer. Nothing called to her.

Just as her day had begun, she couldn't stop thinking about her mother. If Eryk hadn't fired her, what could he have said to make her go to such lengths to disguise the truth?

Claire didn't know – and she planned to find out – but in the meantime, at least she had cream cakes.

CHAPTER FOUR

*C*laire spent Sunday alone in her shop, working on her fresh linen scent. As enjoyable as she always found the experimenting phase, her mother was never far from her mind.

On Monday morning, she awoke with a plan. The first move of a plan, at least. And as soon as she clarified one detail, she felt certain the rest would fall into place.

After everything was set up for the day, she left Damon to look after the shop and visited the post office two doors down.

Even though the sign still advertised the place as Northash Post Office, it had been a long time since that was the sole aim of the business. Now, it was more of a corner shop selling newspapers, cigarettes, alcohol, and confectionary, and the post office half of the business was limited to a single booth.

Janet wasn't in her usual spot behind the booth's clear plastic window, and Leo wasn't behind the shop counter. Instead, a man she only vaguely recognised stood behind the counter, flicking through a ring binder.

Scanning the chocolate bars, Claire glanced at him. Suited men in their mid-to-late forties didn't frequent her shop often, which made them even more memorable when they showed up.

This one had rushed in right before closing last Friday. She'd never learned his name, but she remembered the candle. He'd picked his purchase based on the label without bothering to smell anything and made a joke about it being a last-minute gift. He'd gone for last month's rose petal star candle, the most romantic of her offerings.

"Just these, please," she said, putting a selection of chocolate bars on the counter as she looked past the man to the back room's open door. "Is Janet about?"

"Janet?" he asked, standing in front of the till, his finger on his chin. "Is that the post office woman?"

"And my mother, amongst other things."

"Oh, then she's not turned up."

He stabbed a button on the till and the drawer shot

out. He didn't bother checking the amount of money she handed over, though luckily, she'd given him the exact change. After closing it with his hip, he flipped to the front of the ring binder. Eyes scanned the page until his finger found what he was looking for.

"Looks like her Monday shifts have been crossed out."

Decades of regularity in Janet's shifts at the post office had made it easy for Claire to forget all about the recent slashing of her mother's Monday shift. Like last night, she'd bemoaned Eryk's penny-pinching business tactics when he'd made the decision earlier in the year.

"My mistake," Claire said. "Are you new here?"

"Technically, no," he said, closing the binder. "Although, this is my first day *working* here. Trying to figure out the ropes. Eryk was my business partner."

"Then I'm sorry for your loss."

"Thank you." He offered a smile. "You never expect to get a phone call like that. So senseless. So random. He was a good man, like a brother to me."

"I never knew Eryk only part-owned this place."

Through the open door to the stock room, Claire noticed movement. Was that Leo? She'd hoped to speak with him too.

"He was the majority owner," he explained,

checking a chunky gold wristwatch. "He was thirty percent short when this place went on the market five years back. The man had only been in the country a month at that point. Had ambition I'd only seen in myself, so I covered the shortfall for a small slice. He said he was going to own this village, and I believed him." He chuckled, his down-turned brows souring the happiness as he stared at nothing. "I can't believe he's gone."

Before Claire could offer her condolences once again, the door to the back swung inwards, and Tomek emerged, carrying a stack of boxes. Two days ago, when she hadn't known his name, he'd been screaming for help over his father's body. Now, he seemed to be working.

DI Ramsbottom's comment about Eryk 'showing him the ropes' the morning of the shooting popped into her mind.

"I'm sorry about what happened to your father," she offered on her way out.

"Do I know you?" he asked bluntly, his eyes as pale as his father's.

"I-I own the candle shop two doors down," she said, nodding through the wall. "I was here on Saturday when everything happened."

"Oh." He returned his attention to the shelves. "Thanks. I'll miss him. He was like a best friend."

"Not *all* the time," the man behind the counter called out. "You two had your moments, let's not forget."

"So what, Duncan?" said Tomek. "He was on better speaking terms with me than Berna when he died."

The electronic buzzer above the door rang and Leo pushed his way in, gaze already on the floor. The black eye he'd sported on Saturday had begun to yellow around the edges.

"Hi, Claire," he said in a small voice as he rushed past.

"Hi, Leo."

"*There* you are!" Duncan slapped the counter before checking his watch again. "I said you could have an extra hour's lie-in, not half the morning off."

"Sorry, Dad."

"You're here now." He swapped places with Leo. "I need to get to the lawyers to see how things are going to work without Eryk here. I honestly have no idea where I stand or what I'm supposed to be doing. Will you two be alright on your own?"

"We'll manage," Tomek said, joining Leo behind the counter. "Won't we, Leo?"

Leo jumped as Tomek's hand slapped down on his

shoulder. He nodded, which was apparently enough for Duncan to make his way to the door.

"I thought I recognised you," Duncan said as he passed Claire. "Would have given you a discount if you'd said we were neighbours."

Another buzz announced Duncan's departure. As soon as he was gone, Tomek whispered something to Leo before giving him another pat and slinking into the back room.

Instead of leaving with her chocolate, Claire approached the counter again.

"Your eye looks sore."

"Oh." His fingers touched the edge as though he'd forgotten it was there. "Fell over walking down the stairs. Hit my face on the bannister."

Claire nodded her understanding, though she'd expected him to say the gunman had taken a swing at him. If he had, she might not have thought more of it – but how many people gave themselves black eyes as purple and yellow as Leo's with a little trip down the stairs?

"I'm sorry about what you went through on Friday," she said, resting her hand on his. "From what I've heard, it was a real ordeal."

Leo jerked his hands away and tucked them into his armpits. Stepping back, Claire wondered what she'd done wrong. Her mother had always joked that, based on how flustered he got whenever Claire came in, Leo seemed to be nursing a crush despite the age gap between them. She'd seen it too; the young man's nervous disposition made him easy to read.

Today, he couldn't even look Claire in the eye.

"I didn't know your dad part-owned this place."

"It's how I got the job."

"Explains why you put up with my mum," she said with a smile. "I don't suppose you know if she'll be in tomorrow?"

"She should be," he said with a shrug. "Don't see why not."

"Are you talking about that post office *witch*?" Tomek called from the back room before walking into the shop, his phone pressed to his ear. "Because she won't be in *any* time. One of the last things my dad did was fire her, and I'm not going to let that go undone just because he's dead."

"I suspected as much," Claire said. "Do you know why?"

"How long have you got?" Tomek scoffed. "Dad was always complaining about her. Rude, stuck-up, difficult to work with. Before Duncan offered up Leo, we couldn't keep anyone on the books past their trial period … and do you know why? Because your mother scared them off."

"Alright, Tom," Leo whispered, glancing at Claire. His cheeks flushed with embarrassment. "It's her mum. She worked here for forty years."

"I don't care." Tomek's pale eyes gave Claire a once-over. "Her mother committed fraud."

"Fraud?"

"That's what I said," he snapped, slapping both hands on the counter. "Your mum doesn't work here anymore, okay? I'm in charge now. So, unless you're going to buy anything else, you can stick your questions and condolences and get back to selling your stinking candles."

Claire stifled a laugh, more amused by the young man's arrogance than anything. Twenty, DI Ramsbottom had said, and yet he spoke with the confidence of a seasoned professional. Eryk had been the same way. Considering the freshness of Tomek's grief, she swallowed the urge to give him a piece of her mind.

"How about a drink over lunch?" Claire asked Leo. "My treat?"

Tomek's fingers wrapped around Leo's shoulder again.

"Another time?" he replied with a waxen half-smile. "Not really in the mood today."

"Completely understand," she said, smiling at him and ignoring Tomek's glare. "You know where I am, okay? If you ever want that drink … or a friendly chat. I'll let you get back to work."

Reluctantly, Claire left the young men alone. Her instincts had been right about her mother's firing. After only a brief interaction, she felt certain the gut feeling she'd had in The Park Inn would also be correct.

Something didn't quite line up.

"*Claire?*"

Dressed head to toe in her usual vibrant clothes, Em, a yoga instructor at the gym Ryan managed, jogged over. Despite her tattoo-drenched skin, she'd taken on a golden tan since Claire had seen her the week before.

"What's going on around here?" Em asked as she looked around the square. "Took the narrowboat down to Lancaster after your mother's party was cancelled. As soon as I moored up, I sensed the energy was all off-kilter."

"Then you won't know what happened."

"It's something terrible, isn't it?" Em rested her

fingers against her lips. "I can feel it. It's not your mother's food poisoning—"

"No, she's fine," Claire insisted, knowing her mother would be pleased by her choice of descriptor. "Eryk Kowalski. Someone shot him at the post office. He didn't make it."

"Kowalski?" Em gasped. "I think his wife and daughter are in my yoga class. They're from Poland, aren't they?"

"That's them," she said. "I just had the dubious pleasure of meeting Eryk's son, Tomek."

"That's a name I *do* know," she said. "His mother, Anna, talks of him often when she's seeking spiritual counsel from me. The poor family. How did it happen?"

"Random burglary, apparently."

"Only apparently?"

"I-I'm not convinced," she admitted. "The night before he died, Eryk fired my mother. She's been lying about it, but Tomek just confirmed it. He said … he said she committed *fraud.*"

"Oh, dear." Em shook her head. "That doesn't sound like something your mother would do."

"Neither does having Eryk shot over an alleged argument," Claire whispered, looking around the quiet square, "but that theory has already whizzed around the place. I'm trying to clear Mum's name." She paused and looked back at the post office. "I don't know if I'm way off, but Leo seems scared of Tomek."

"I don't want to break her confidence, but that lines up with how Anna talks of her son. Quite the agitator in their family. At my last class, she seemed quite distraught about something he'd said to Eryk, but she didn't go into detail. They're a very tight-knit family. Private."

Benefit of the doubt or not, the cruelty in his stare hinted at a more permanent character trait than one caused by grief. If her father's suggestion that it could be an inside job was on the right track, Tomek had just shot to the top of the list of suspects.

"What classes do the mother and daughter duo usually attend?" asked Claire.

"Mondays and Wednesdays without fail," Em said with a look towards the gym, "though considering what they've just been through, I doubt I'll see them for a while."

"If they show up tonight, can you..." She stopped herself saying 'drop me a text message' when she remembered Em's phone usage stretched to the red phone box outside the pub. "Can you ask Ryan to call me? I'd quite like to talk to them."

"Consider it done. It's about time you joined one of my classes. I've been asking you for months."

"Well, I never said—"

"You'll enjoy it," Em interrupted with a wink. "Trust me."

Em said her farewells, leaving Claire to return to the shop. Most Monday mornings in the square were slow, so there weren't any customers quite yet, though it was worth opening for the random rushes they might get later in the day.

Still, she didn't condone falling asleep at the counter.

"You're fired!" she cried, clapping her hands sharply.

Damon shot up, an order form stuck to his cheek. He blinked around the shop through glasses sitting askew on the bridge of his nose.

"Sorry, late night playing *Dawn Ship 2* online with Sean." He stifled a yawn as he straightened his glasses. "Wait, did you just *fire* me?"

"Yes, with no warnings." She smirked. "We were right about Eryk firing my mum. I straight up asked her last night, and she lied to my face, but Eryk's brat of a son just confirmed it."

"What did she do?"

"Apparently she was rude and difficult to work

with."

"That's nothing new."

"What if I throw some fraud in the mix?"

"*Fraud?*" Damon laughed, though it faded out when Claire didn't join in. "Oh, right. That doesn't sound like your mother. Shame Eryk isn't here to ask. We could crack out the Ouija board?"

"Sounds easier than trying to get it from my mother." She straightened the samples on display next to the till. "Why is she trying so hard to pretend nothing is happening?"

"Embarrassment?" he suggested, sipping the coffee she'd made him nearly an hour ago even though it had to be stone cold by now. "Though, if she really committed fraud, surely Eryk would have gone to the police?"

"That's a good point," she said. "How do you feel about having our first work outing tonight?"

"Like, a night out?" Damon's eyes lit up. "Manchester or—"

"Actually," she interjected before he could get his hopes up. "I was thinking more a yoga class."

"I feel the same way about that as I do about you firing me." He squinted. "Since when are you into yoga?"

"Since I found out Eryk's wife and daughter attend

Em's classes."

"You're doing that face again," Damon said, circling his finger. "You look all determined."

"Is that such a bad thing?"

"It freaks me out," he said, pushing up his glasses. "I thought you were only trying to clear your mother's name?"

"I am." She shrugged. "Eryk's wife and daughter might know about this fraud accusation, that's all."

"Keep telling yourself that."

"If it's a random burglary, like DI Ramsbottom seems to think, hopefully he'll soon prove it." Claire reached into her pocket and tossed the chocolate bars she'd bought onto the counter. "Now, shut up, or I'll fire you for real."

"I'm shaking in my boots, boss."

Claire couldn't fathom ever having a real reason to fire Damon … but she'd never imagined anyone firing her mother, either. Peeling the purple foil off a crumbly Twirl bar, the implications of what 'fraud' her mother could have committed scratched at her every thought.

"You were joking about the yoga class, right?" asked Damon.

"Oh," said Claire around a mouthful of chocolate, "absolutely not."

CHAPTER FIVE

"*E*veryone is looking," Damon muttered, crossing his arms in front of his body as he half-hid behind Claire. "I've never felt more uncomfortable."

"You look fine." She lunged, but the crotch of the pink and yellow linen trousers still didn't give. "Although Em's idea of baggy is my idea of barely fitting."

"At least you got a t-shirt." He edged further behind Claire. "Some people shouldn't wear vests, and *I'm* one of them."

"We spent half our lives in the same lumpy jumpsuits at the factory."

"They left a *lot* to the imagination."

"No one is looking."

Claire wished that weren't a lie.

Everyone *was* looking. She wasn't sure if they were judgemental or just curious about the newcomers to their yoga class. Damon and Claire certainly stuck out in their borrowed clothes, but they were far from wearing the wildest outfits.

Half the class were women in skin-tight bra tops and leggings, while the other half were decked out in finery even whackier than Em's. There weren't many rooms in which Em's daily outfits wouldn't be the most eye-catching, but in this one, she ended up somewhere on the simple end of the spectrum.

Damon and Claire sandwiched themselves between an older woman decorated in beads, rings, and bracelets, and a lady with the biggest hair Claire had ever seen. Both offered warm smiles. The woman with the jewellery clattered as she put her hands into prayer and nodded.

"Namaste," she said.

"You too," Damon replied, moving closer to Claire. "One wrong move and these shorts are going to split, I swear. I hate you, Claire. I hate you so much."

"We don't *hate* here," Em announced as she strode to her position in the corner of her yoga area. In the mirrored walls, two more Ems appeared. "For the next hour, we simply be. We choose love, and we let go. By the end of my class, Damon, I daresay you'll have experienced a transformation that will make you wonder why you didn't come sooner." Em shot a playful smile at Claire. "Same to you, my dear friend."

"I still hate you," Damon whispered, resisting the natural separation as people laid out their mats. "After this, you owe me that staff night out."

"Deal." She laid out two pink mats. Once Damon took his, Claire copied the arm-flinging stretches happening around them. "Now pay attention. Remember why we're here."

"And so, we begin." Em inhaled, her eyes closing as her hands went into prayer pose, prompting everyone bar Claire and Damon to copy. "And now, down into Child's Pose."

After catching Ryan's tickled expression in the mirrors from where he watched from across the gym, Claire did her best to ignore him and follow those around her. Being such a beginner, she didn't feel too bad about staring. As much as she was mimicking their moves, she was trying to figure out who Eryk's wife and daughter were.

After easily dismissing half the group, only two women around Eryk's age and three about the right age for a daughter remained. Identical pale hair and eyes gave the women away long before Claire saw them interact during a short break midway through the class.

"You're doing very well," Em said, drifting to Claire and Damon as the order of the class melted away into groups. "A little distracted, but I see the effort."

"What about me?" Damon asked after gulping water.

"Damon…" Em grinned as she took him in, clearly trying to find a compliment. "You look like you're having *fun*!"

"Yeah," he agreed, wiping sweat from his brow. "Maybe."

Watching through the mirror, Claire noticed the mother and daughter duo drift to the row of lockers at the back of the gym. Next to the lockers, Ryan trained a man on an elliptical machine.

"You're doing great, Pete!" Ryan encouraged. "Another two minutes and you've crushed this workout."

Seeing Ryan in his enthusiastic work mode was always strange. He'd been so shy around her lately. Here, in his element, he had an easy, confident glow that made Claire smile.

"Am I making a fool of myself?" she asked him, keeping one eye on the women at the lockers.

"No more than usual," he said with a grin. "You're

doing great. Is Damon alright? He keeps tugging at his shorts."

"Ah, yes." Claire patted Ryan's stomach, still surprised by the feeling of abs under her fingertips. "Your and Em's idea of baggy clothes doesn't quite line up with what we're used to."

Ryan laughed as he helped his wobbly legged victim off the torture device. As casually as she could, Claire dropped into a lunge. Swapping feet, she took a long step and lunged again until she was in earshot of the two women.

"Berna, I *told* you," the older woman whispered as they rooted through their bags in their side-by-side lockers, "I'm going home as soon as possible, and you're coming with me."

"And *I* told *you*, I'm staying here." Berna's hand rested on her midsection. "I have bigger things to think about now."

"It's what your father wanted."

"And what about what *I* want?"

"You don't know what you want," Anna snapped. "You're still a child. Everything we want is in Poland. Our friends, our family."

"Everything *you* want."

The young woman slammed her locker door and breezed past Claire to the yoga mats.

"Berna!"

Not wanting to linger, Claire lunged away, shaking her arms out as she reached Damon. Sat cross-legged on her mat, Berna looked like she was fighting back tears as her fingers tapped away on her phone.

"That's Berna, Eryk's daughter," she told Damon. "Sounds like her father was trying to send her to Poland." As Claire stretched her calves, she looked at the lockers again. "The woman with the red flower in her hair is Anna, her mother. Apparently, she's in a rush to get back to Poland and wants to take her daughter with her, but Berna has different ideas."

"Who *are* you?" he whispered. "What does any of that have to do with finding out about your mother's supposed fraud? Just *ask* them."

"I will," she whispered back. "But it's nice to have some background information."

"You're like a machine."

The second half of the class advanced to the point Claire couldn't fake her way through the moves. As the surrounding women bent and twisted through Lotus to Firefly and into the painful-looking backbend of King Pigeon, Claire and Damon bowed out. With all the panting and huffing between them, all attempts at grace were futile, and it felt kinder to stop embarrassing themselves.

"You made the first half easier," Claire said to Em as the class finally packed up.

"Perhaps a little. I don't like to scare people off with the more complicated moves right away, though there are more challenging moves than the ones you saw."

"Head spinning and levitation?"

Em chuckled. "That's my next class."

Someone behind Claire laughed, and they turned to see Berna rolling up her mat.

"Sorry," she said to Claire, still laughing. "I didn't mean to eavesdrop, but that's the first thing that's made me laugh since…"

Em backed away, her smile saying, 'I'll leave you to it.'

"I'm not sure I'm cut out for this," Claire admitted.

"First time?"

"That obvious?"

"You did good," she said as she stood. "You should have seen me at the first class my mother dragged me to. Couldn't even touch my toes."

Despite her breathy laugh, sadness clouded her icy eyes. She and Tomek had to be close in age, though Berna had an air of maturity that her brother lacked.

"I know it doesn't help," Claire offered before Berna drifted away, "but I'm sorry about what happened."

"Thank you," she said, letting down her long blonde hair from a ponytail. "If Em has taught me anything, it's the importance of human connection, so it does help. I'm sorry about what happened too. I feel as though I'm wandering around in a daze to stop myself breaking down." Her eyes glazed over and then immediately snapped back. "I'm over-sharing. I shouldn't be transferring my energies to you like this."

"You don't have to apologise," she said. "I've done my fair bit of over-sharing in my time. Dealing with these things is never easy."

"*These things*," she repeated, her smile tightening. "Death is such an ugly topic of conversation these days. Unavoidable, and yet we avoid it like it's not coming for everyone. In Poland, when I was fourteen, my grandmother died. There, we mourned. We welcomed the sadness and faced our darkness. Here, we must keep calm and carry on."

Berna's eyes cut across to her mother, who was talking to Em as she organised the yoga mats.

"I'm afraid that's one of our British flaws."

"You could say that, yes." Berna stared at her mother until flicking her gaze back to Claire. "How did you know my father?"

"My mother works for him," she said. "Or should I say *worked*. He fired her on Friday."

"Ah, the *problem* woman," Berna said, "as my father called her."

"She has her flaws too," Claire admitted. "Bottling up the bad stuff being one of them. She's the walking embodiment of keep calm and carry on, I'm afraid. I don't suppose you have any idea why your father fired her?"

"I'm not involved with the post office," she said. "But I think it was something to do with pensions."

"Your brother said fraud earlier."

"Yes, that too," she said. "And I'm sorry you had the displeasure of talking to my brother. Even in grief, he's still a brat."

"I … noticed."

"Perfect clone of my father." Berna's top lip curled as her hand drifted to her midsection and dropped away just as quickly. "I'm sorry I don't know more about your mother. And I'm sorry for referring to her as a *problem*. My father's words. He's always had an issue with confident women."

"Oh, I'm related to her, and I'd say his assessment probably wasn't too far off," Claire confessed behind her hand. "She has her moments."

"Don't we all." Berna's eyes fixed on her mother again. As she drifted away, she said, "It was nice talking with you…?"

"Claire." She extended a hand. "Nice to meet you, Berna."

"I didn't tell you my name," she replied with a curious smile, shaking Claire's hand.

"Tomek mentioned you," Claire said quickly, her cheeks firing up. "Put two and two together when I realised you were Eryk's daughter."

Berna nodded, but her enquiring gaze lingered on Claire for what felt like an age before she walked away. Claire didn't breathe until Berna left the yoga area.

With Damon changing in the men's, Claire retreated to the women's changing rooms, smiling awkwardly at those changing semi-nude on the benches. Claire took a cubicle and relieved herself of the outfit she'd borrowed from Em. After rolling on some deodorant, she climbed into her familiar clothes and back to normality.

When she'd finished, the locker room had emptied, though echoed conversation floated from the open shower block.

"Come with me," the echo said. "A new life. The fresh start you keep talking about. Promise me you'll think about it."

Claire fussed with her hair in the mirror, ears straining to catch the next part.

"As soon as we can," the echo continued. "I don't want to stay here any longer than necessary."

As Claire applied lip balm, Eryk's widow came around the shower wall, fully dressed and dropping her phone into her handbag. Claire smiled at her through the mirror, but Anna didn't return it.

"Have fun?" Ryan asked, leaning on a calf weight machine as she exited the bathroom. "You should come more often."

"You sound like my mother."

"I didn't mean it in the same way your mother does," he whispered, pushing a stray hair from her glasses. "Exercise can be a good release, that's all."

"I will admit, I felt myself getting in *the zone*. Just don't tell Em or she'll have me at every lesson. I'm not sure my body will ever be able to do a King Pigeon."

"Anything is possible," he said. "Still on for Amelia's birthday tea party tomorrow?"

"Wouldn't miss it. Though I think you can count the rest of my family out. Not sure I can put up with my mother's current energy at a kid's party."

Ryan pressed a goodbye kiss on her cheek. After waving to Em, Claire left through the sliding doors. She found Damon outside, leaning against the old library frontage of the converted gym.

"I think there's only one way to follow up a yoga

class," Damon said, kicking away from the wall. "Pint at the pub?"

"If you insist."

"You're buying," he said. "You owe me after that public humiliation."

"Fair."

While Claire didn't enjoy the extra sweating that came with summer days, she loved the evenings. The slight breeze that still carried a hint of humidity in the warmth. With the walls of the square blocking most of the gentle wind, it was easy to pretend they were in a more tropical location than North West England.

"It wasn't *that* humiliating, was it?" Claire asked as she joined Damon at a picnic table in the softly lit beer garden in front of the pub. "My mother would have called that 'putting yourself out there'. You never know – it might be a better way to meet new people than the dating apps."

They took their first sips of Hesketh Homebrew and breathed sighs of relief.

"I've deleted the apps."

"Again?" Claire took another quick drink. "You were only just back on them."

"They're no good," he said with a shrug. "It's like online shopping, but all you get are dry conversations and red flags everywhere."

"I can't argue with that."

"And who says I need to be on them, anyway?" His brows went up as his finger circled the rim of his glass. "I meet people all the time."

"Are you trying to subtly hint that you're seeing someone, Damon Gilbert?"

He pushed up his glasses and sipped his pint.

"You *are*!" Claire whispered, slapping his arm. "How *dare* you and *not* tell *me*!"

"It's not like that," he whispered back. "It's complicated."

"Does she know you exist?"

"Yes."

"Does she know you like her?"

"Who said there's someone?"

"Your red cheeks." Claire gave one a pinch. "I can't believe you're being secretive with me right now."

"I'm not," he said with a laugh. "It's just … *complicated*. It won't go anywhere. I'm probably picking up on flirting that isn't even happening." He lifted his glass, and before it reached his lips, he said, "And anyway, we're not here to talk about my love life or lack thereof. I saw you talking to the daughter. Did you find out what led to your mother's current employment status?"

"Something to do with pensions."

"Pension fraud? What's that when it's at home?"

"I'm not sure," she admitted, looking across the square to the post office. The only light came from the flat above it. "She didn't say anything, but I think Berna might be pregnant."

"What does that have to do with your mother's sacking?"

"Nothing," Claire replied, offering a shrug, "but it's a great motive for murder."

"*Random* burglary."

"I know, I know." She wafted a hand dismissively. "Doesn't take away from the fact that it is, though. The police will probably have answers by the morning."

"And if they don't?"

"A little civilian investigation never hurt anyone," she said, scanning the quiet village square. "The dating apps aren't the only places with red flags right now."

CHAPTER SIX

"These are good," Sally remarked as she flicked through the crispy sheets filled with watercolour paintings. "Why's he working in a gym when he can paint like this?"

Sipping her cider, Claire pulled away from the work-in-progress on Ryan's easel. She joined Sally on the other side of the art studio as children's laughter and bubbly music floated through the cellar ceiling.

"Ryan doesn't think he's all that good."

"How can he not?" Sally pulled out a painting of a delicate pink rose bouquet. "I'd hang most of these in any house I was trying to sell. What a shame to have them hidden in a cardboard box down in the basement."

"He didn't pick up a paintbrush all those years he

lived in Spain," Claire said. "I think it reminded him too much of his mum."

"She taught him to paint?"

"Paula was an amazing artist." Claire remembered with a smile. "He only started again once he moved back home."

"Forget show homes." Sally swapped the paintings for her red wine. "If he lets me, I might buy one for wherever I end up."

"How's the house hunt going?"

"Middling." She sighed. "You'd think I'd be able to find somewhere considering it's my job. Turns out being an estate agent makes every viewing a hunt for the cracks and damp I usually try to hypnotise people into not seeing."

"At least you've still got the house."

"Can't move until that sells, anyway." Sally sipped her wine. "I'm hoping for a quick sale. If it weren't for keeping things normal for the girls, I wouldn't even have gone back. Too many bad memories." Standing in front of the easel, Sally took in the half-finished clock tower painting. "Paul's all settled in his new place. Swanky Manchester penthouse just 'round the corner from his new firm. Screams of a midlife crisis cliché, but he seems to be doing alright."

"What about you, mate?"

"Oh, I'm well shot of him." Sally laughed. "Ever since he stopped spitting his dummy out, the divorce has been hurtling along. Had I known it would be this easy, I would have left him years ago. If he wants to live in a city and like pictures of tight twenty-two-year-old fitness models on Instagram all day, he can be my guest."

"Please tell me you're not still stalking him online."

"Only once a week," she said airily. "Better than once an hour."

"True."

"*And* I get somewhere to ship the kids to a few nights a week." Sally's wine clinked Claire's cider in a toast. "I love them, but I don't know how Ryan does the full-time parenting thing on his own. That Friday night to Monday morning stretch on my own has been *bliss*."

Sally moved in closer, glancing up at the ceiling as the party cheered; someone must have won pass the parcel.

"Speaking of divorce," she whispered. "Any news from what's-her-face?"

"Maya," Claire replied, equally hushed, "and no. Nothing yet."

"Unbelievable." Sally clutched her wine to her

chest. "What sort of mother leaves and forgets she has two children?"

Claire shrugged. Ryan rarely talked about his estranged wife, Maya – not that she could blame him. They'd lived together and raised their children in Spain for years, until she ran off with Ryan's friend, never to be heard from again.

"Do you think she'll show her face?" Sally pushed. "You'd have thought her daughter's tenth birthday would have been enough to bring her crawling out of the woodwork."

"She has to, doesn't she?" asked Claire. "Like you said, two kids. She won't stay away forever, and Ryan is still technically *married* to her."

"Let's hope it doesn't change things between you two if she does show up."

"I think it's more of *when* not if."

"Well, she's not here now." Sally toasted her glass again. "What's the latest with you, anyway? Anything to report?"

"If you mean have we kissed yet, then no."

"Still?"

"Still."

Claire scanned the studio. It had been a homemade casino when the house belonged to her Uncle Pat. When she'd helped Ryan paint the dark walls to their current bright white, they'd almost kissed … and yet, nothing since.

Kisses on the cheek? Yes.

Never the lips.

"Maybe you need to be the one to do it?" Sally suggested as she rummaged through a basket of half-squeezed paint tubes. "Just grab him and snog him like you would if you were sixteen again."

"We never kissed when we were sixteen."

"But you wanted to." Sally winked. "Have you told him—"

"That I fell in love with him two decades ago?" Claire shook her head. "Don't be silly. As far as Ryan knows, we're on the same fresh page. I don't want to freak him out. It's too much baggage."

"Two kids and an estranged wife? I don't think you're the one with…"

Sally's voice trailed off as the door at the top of the staircase opened. Ryan ducked to look at them.

"So, this is where you're hiding," he said, motioning for them to come back.

"There's only so many times I can do the Cha Cha Slide and the Macarena," Sally said as she left the cellar. "Suppose I should make sure the girls aren't ripping each other's hair out. I'll leave you to it."

Ryan stuck to the wall as Sally passed him. He took

the final few steps down to the studio, his yellow party hat still perched on his head.

"This is excellent," she said, motioning to the clock painting.

"You think?" He scratched at the back of his neck. "I wasn't sure if the light source made any sense, so I gave up on it."

Ryan leaned in. For a split second, she thought he had chosen this moment to finally kiss her, but he looked up at the ceiling and whispered, "Your parents are here."

Claire immediately hurried upstairs. Assuming they wouldn't attend, given the circumstances, she hadn't called to check.

But there they were, taking their shoes off in the hallway and carrying a bag filled with presents. She looked around them for a flash of black fabric.

"Don't worry, little one," said her father as he hung up his jacket, "your grandmother is at home taking a nap."

"Went up to see the factory," Janet said, fluffing her hair in the hall mirror. "We could have driven, but she *insisted* we walk. Spent the last hour complaining about how exhausted she was from all the exercise."

"Why did you go up there?"

"She wanted to see it," said Janet. "Apparently, she used to work there, which was news to me."

"Grandmother Moreen worked at the candle factory?" Claire arched a brow. "She's never mentioned that before."

"In her early twenties," added Alan. "She probably doesn't want people thinking she was ever a lowly factory worker and not born a teacher of physical education."

Presents in hand, Janet joined the hyperactive children and few adults in the front room. Sally and Damon whispered to each other in one corner; the other lingering parents stood opposite.

Amelia, now ten years old, seemed determined to beat Sally's daughter, Ellie, also aged ten, at musical chairs. Ryan's son, seven-year-old Hugo, was on his handheld games console in the corner. Sally's eight-year-old daughter, Aria, watched over his shoulder. There were a few other children from Amelia's school, but according to Ryan, she hadn't made many friends since joining Northash Primary.

"Any progress on the case?" Alan whispered as they watched the party from the hallway.

"Confirmed that Mum has been fired," Claire replied, "and that's straight from Tomek's mouth. The daughter confirmed it too. Something to do with fraud and pensions."

"*Fraud*?" Alan pulled Claire out of view of the door. "You can't be serious?"

"That's what they're saying."

"She went to work this morning," he murmured. "Within twenty minutes, she was back, and she wouldn't talk about it. Despite the façade right now, she's not well. She's never shut me out like this before."

"Maybe we need to confront her together?" she suggested, glancing over her shoulder towards the party. "Speaking of Eryk's kids, I overheard his wife yesterday. Seems like she's in a rush to go back to Poland and take her daughter with her. I know Ramsbottom thinks it's random—"

"Not anymore," he interrupted, rubbing his hand across his jaw. "Met up with Harry in Marley's for lunch. He's changed his tune. There's no security camera footage of the burglar."

"Was he invisible?"

"The cameras were switched off," he said. "There's nothing whatsoever from that entire day. It could be a coincidence, but Harry doesn't seem to think so. He tried talking to Tomek and Leo again, but Tomek has vanished into thin air."

"Has he done a runner?"

"It's looking that way."

"If someone purposefully switched off the cameras it points even more to an inside job."

"Can't see it being anything else." Alan glanced down the hall. "I'd go as far as to say that Tomek and Leo's original statements are useless. Someone switched off those cameras, which means they knew what they were doing. They had to have worked there or been close to someone who did to know. With Tomek missing from the picture, he's the likely suspect."

"He certainly had an attitude when I spoke to him," Claire revealed. "Leo seemed scared of him. Could he be lying to cover for Tomek? But would Tomek shoot his own father?"

"I wouldn't like to speculate, but if Tomek isn't behind it, there's only one other reason those two boys would cook up a story."

"They're protecting someone."

"Exactly, little one." He gave her cheek a pat. "You're a chip off the old block; that's exactly what I said to Harry. You were right to trust your instincts about that morning not being—"

"What are you two doing whispering out here?" Janet hissed, popping her head around the doorframe. "If you hadn't noticed, there's a party going on. You're not down in your shed now."

Alan and Claire exchanged a 'that's us told' look before joining everyone else and leaving the case talk behind. The game of musical chairs had ended, and they'd moved onto another round of pass the parcel. If Amelia noticed her mother's absence, her grin hid it well.

While her parents picked at the small buffet under the window, Claire joined Ryan behind the sofa. He wrapped his arm around her and pulled her in.

They might not have properly kissed yet, but even with one of the mothers giving her a 'what's *he* doing with *her*' look, nothing felt more natural than being close to Ryan. Having his arm around her shoulder was something teenage Claire would have killed for.

"*I win!*" Ellie cried, ripping the final sheet of paper off the parcel to reveal a small piece of cardboard. "Oh, cool! A V-Bucks gift voucher!"

"A what now?" Claire asked Ryan.

"Something for *Fortnite*. Don't ask because I don't know." He chuckled. "According to Amelia, putting toys in pass the parcel is *lame*."

"*Dad!*" Amelia cried, running up to him all red-faced. "Adults musical chairs."

"*Yeah!*" some of the other kids agreed.

"You in?" Ryan asked.

"Of course." Claire cracked her neck from side to side. "I've never lost a game of musical chairs to you, and I don't intend to start now."

Alan was the first out, followed quickly by Janet. One by one, the other parents dropped out. Claire found it satisfying to slide into a chair before the woman who had been eyeballing Ryan's arm around her. Damon knocked Ryan out, and despite her best efforts, Sally took the penultimate seat, ejecting Claire from the game.

While Sally and Damon stalked each other around the last remaining chair, their eyes locked. Their grins were even wider than the kids' had been. Claire's smile faltered as she looked around the room.

"Where's Mum?" Claire asked her father.

"She just slipped out," he said from the sofa. "Probably to use the bathroom."

Leaning against the doorframe, Claire listened for the creaky floorboards in the bathroom upstairs. Nothing. She looked down the hall to the kitchen, and though it was empty, she caught the back gate settling into its frame.

Leaving the party, Claire went to the back door. Before she took the three steps down to the small back garden, she spotted her mother in the garden of the end house to the right. Without taking a moment to think about it, Janet scurried up the three steps, knocked, and vanished inside.

"Damon won," Ryan said, slipping his hand around Claire's waist. "Sally's arguing for a rematch."

"Sounds like Sally," she replied, pulling away from the door. "Who lives in the end house?"

"Right now?" He sucked the air through his teeth. "I don't think anyone's moved in since Elsie died. Poor woman. Had a heart attack in Starfall Park last month."

"And you're sure it's empty?"

"I think so," he said with a shrug. "She had a granddaughter living with her, but I haven't seen her around since. Are you thinking of moving out of your flat already?"

"I saw my mum there," she said. "Just now. She knocked, and someone let her in."

"How strange," he said, resting a hand on her shoulder. "Might be squatters?"

"Maybe." Claire closed the back door. "But what does that have to do with my mum?"

Once back in the party, Janet returned a few minutes later with her easy, breezy, 'everything is perfectly normal, so please don't ask' smile plastered from ear to ear. Ten minutes later, she made her excuses and pulled Alan away from the buffet.

Once Claire's parents had left, claiming they needed to return to the cul-de-sac before Moreen awoke from her nap, the guests dropped like flies. An hour later, only Ryan and Sally's kids were running around the house.

"Why don't you two go and have a few hours of *private* time?" Sally suggested as Claire and Ryan washed up together at the kitchen sink. "Damon and I will watch the kids."

"Are you sure?" Ryan asked.

"They'll be bouncing off the walls for hours yet after all that sugar," she said with a reassuring nod. "Besides, my girls are getting on with your two properly for the first time, and it would be a shame to pull them apart when they're having so much fun. Go and have a drink at the pub or something."

"It would be nice," Ryan admitted.

"Yeah," Claire said, winking her thanks at Sally for offering. "I'd like that."

Leaving them all to a game of hide and seek in the house, Claire and Ryan left through the front door as the setting summer sun bled orange over Christ Church Square.

"Glad we get to do this," Ryan said, wrapping his fingers around hers as they walked past Trinity Community Church on the corner of Warton Lane.

"Between work and the kids, we never get much time alone."

"Who knew adulthood would be so busy?" A lump rose in her throat. "How are things?"

"Good," he replied with a shrug. "Work's fine. I enjoy it, actually. Kids are enjoying the summer off school."

"That's great," she said. "I more meant between us, though."

"Oh." His freckled cheeks flushed red. "I-I don't know how to answer that." He paused and asked, "Good? Things are good, aren't they?"

Claire smiled, not minding his shyness so much now.

"Yeah," she squeezed his hand. "You're right. Things are…"

Claire's voice trailed off as they rounded the corner into the main square. Police cars and vans lined the road as a small crowd watched on from the shadow of the clock tower.

"It's a circus," Ryan muttered. "It's not your shop, is it?"

Claire had worried the same thing, but a few more steps showed that her shop was shut and fine.

Two doors down, the post office lights blared into the darkening square as a line of police officers exited the shop. Each carried a rattling box of what sounded like glass bottles that went into the back of a police van. On the corner, Duncan and Leo talked with two officers taking notes.

"Looks like a raid," Ryan whispered as they diverted in the direction of The Hesketh Arms.

"Knock-off alcohol and dodgy cigarettes."

"What?"

"Just something my mum said." Claire shook her head and leaned into Ryan's side. "Doesn't matter."

Before walking through the pub door Ryan had opened for her, she watched as an officer ducked Leo's head into the back of a police car.

Despite her words, Claire couldn't help but think it mattered very much indeed.

CHAPTER SEVEN

*T*he following day, Claire couldn't see her face, but she knew it was green. She didn't get along with Em's narrowboat at the best of times.

This wasn't the best of times.

"I shouldn't have gone for those drinks with Damon," Claire said, clutching the window ledge as the boat gently bobbed. "Damn Damon's timing. Jammy bugger caught me trying to unlock my shop. Couldn't say no when he asked if I wanted to grab a drink."

"Why not?" asked Em.

"Because I'd already had two pints of Hesketh Homebrew with Ryan by that point. Each pint you drink convinces you that you can handle another. It was easier to turn them down when we worked at the factory."

"Having someone else as your boss?"

"Because we couldn't afford it," she said, resting her hand on her stomach. "Minimum wages only go so far."

Em chuckled as she pulled two jars from the small fridge. "How does berry overnight porridge sound?"

"Like a good idea in theory." Claire paused, inhaling a shaky breath. "But in practice? I'm not sure I can handle it right now."

"It was only last week you were starting to get over the water sickness."

"Homebrew has that effect."

"Is that what I'm missing out on?"

"You're better off without it." Claire accepted a glass of cucumber water, her grip weak. "You should have seen us in our twenties. Let's just say we spent our fair share of early shifts swaying at the stickers station. We're practically saints now, compared. Forty." She sipped the water. "I'll get my life together when I'm forty."

"But first, thirty-six." Em crawled across the futon bed heaped with colourful pillows of all textures, her movement rocking the boat. "A little birdie told me your birthday is only a matter of weeks away. Thinking of throwing a party?"

"Oh, don't." Claire pressed her fingers to her mouth. "I can't think about that right now."

"Because of the timing?"

"Because of—"

Claire near leapt over the side of the boat, and not for the first time that morning. Em softly rubbed her back as she created duck food. Dog walkers passed on the other side of the canal, but she couldn't bring herself to so much as glance in their direction.

"If my mother could see me now, she'd kill me. And don't get me started on Grandmother Moreen. I've never seen her drink anything stronger than tomato juice."

"You're a young woman." Em laughed, handing Claire the cucumber water glass. "Mornings of regret usually mean you were living in the moment to get there, and that's fine by me. Just maybe *one* less next time."

"There is no next time," Claire said, though this was a promise she'd made many a time before. "But you were right about the timing. With everything going on at the post office and with my mother, the last thing anyone needs is a party."

"And how is your mother?" Em asked, settling Claire on the edge of the futon. "Has she opened up?"

"Shut down, more like," she admitted, feeling better after emptying her stomach. "I'm really worried about her, Em. She lied about being fired and won't say why. Also, she turned up at Amelia's party about half an hour after you left. And I don't think she was there for the jelly and ice cream. She snuck out of the party and went into a house in Ryan's square that he swears is empty."

"It sounds like your mother is in great pain and turmoil right now." Em sighed, her brows sinking as though she were feeling the same thing. "Did being at my class not prove helpful?"

"Berna added pensions into the fraud," she said. "And Ryan said an old woman used to live in the house my mum went into."

"Elsie Tanner," Em said with a nod, a sad smile lifting her cheeks. "Mrs Tanner. She was my art teacher in high school. Kind woman. Giving spirit. She—"

A dog's bark from deep in the forest on the other side of the canal cut Em off.

"That'll be the police," said Em. "They've been up and down the forest nonstop since they found that gun."

Claire gazed at the forest, catching the glimmer of bright morning sun bouncing off the reflective bits of the officers' uniforms.

"Has Anna mentioned to you that she's in a rush to go home to Poland?" Claire said, taking the shift to the yoga class.

"Frequently." Cross-legged again, Em unscrewed her overnight porridge and skimmed off the top with a large spoon. "In fact, it's the thing she's talked about the most. She never wanted to come to the UK. That was Eryk. He dreamed of business, and she dreams of her family. Some people have a great kinship with their motherland, and I've always felt that from Anna. She misses home dearly."

"Enough to kill Eryk?"

"Now, I never said that." With a twinkle in her eye, Em pointed the spoon at Claire. "But I assume your bright mind knows something I don't if you're asking such a leading question."

Claire paused as two excited dogs met on the waterside path and their owners ground to a halt. They pulled the dogs apart by their leads and went in separate directions, but Claire moved a little closer to Em, all the same.

"Someone cut the cameras at the post office," she revealed in a whisper. "The whole thing was planned. It had to be. And if it wasn't someone who worked there—"

"It was someone close to them." Em airy voice took

on a serious edge. "Yes, I understand why you asked. There's a clear motive there."

"Berna too," she said. "I *think* she might be pregnant, and her father was trying to send her back to Poland. The two might not be connected."

"You're astute, Claire." Em smiled, blinking slowly. "You're absolutely right. That's something else Anna spoke about at length. They are connected. Eryk was deeply traditional, and he wanted Berna to marry before bringing a child into this world." She jabbed her spoon into her oats but didn't pull it out. "There's something else. You've given me some context."

Claire's ears pricked up.

"For what?" she asked, edging closer.

"It might be nothing," she started, digging her large spoon into her breakfast. "A few weeks before Eryk died, perhaps three, I overheard something I shouldn't have. Anna was talking on the phone, and I heard a part of her conversation."

"Shower block?"

"Yes."

"I think someone needs to tell her that even whispers echo in a room full of tiles," she said. "I heard her asking someone to go to Poland with her. Talking about new starts. Sounded pretty romantic."

"Then perhaps we overheard her talking to the

same man." Em inhaled heavily. "I thought she was talking to Eryk until she used his name in a way that made it obvious she was talking *about* him."

"How so?"

"She was talking about Eryk's life insurance," she said darkly. "It was all up to date, apparently. There's a great possibility it's purely coincidental."

"And there's a chance it isn't."

"I've betrayed her confidence," Em said, sinking into the mattress, "but you'd already figured out much of that yourself, and when murder's involved right on our doorstep, it's no time for secrets."

Claire stuck around as long as her stomach could take, which wasn't much longer. Watching Em eat gloopy berry oats combined with the ear-ringing dog barking drove her back onto land.

"Talk to your mother," Em ordered with a hug. "She won't reach out, but she needs you now more than ever."

After promising she would, Claire walked the short way down the path and rounded the corner at The Hesketh Arms. She glanced at the beer garden, now filled with people eating their greasy breakfast fry-ups in the sun. How many hours ago had she ducked behind one side of a picnic table, whizzing beermats at Damon doing the same on the other.

At least she'd given him the owed staff night out.

Knowing she needed food, and content that Damon was dealing with the few customers across the square, Claire stepped up into Marley's Café, the first shop on one of the square's many snaking side streets.

Marley's husband, Eugene, was among the handful of customers. Instead of a slice of cake and a coffee, he had a glass with a fizzing tablet and a familiar, heavy-lidded look of shame.

Singing blurred in Claire's ears.

Echoes of *her* voice.

And Eugene's voice

And why were they on the pool table?

Too embarrassed to meet his weary eyes as he watched the tablet turn the water orange, Claire hurried to the counter.

"Anything that's light on the stomach?" Claire asked, glancing at the display case of vegan cakes. "I'm a little green around the gills today."

"You're not the only one." Marley nodded at Eugene. "Karaoke on the pool table, wasn't it?"

"They can't *contain* me, dear," Eugene groaned with none of his usual theatrics. "Believe me, they've tried. Anyway, blame Claire. It was *her* idea."

"Was it?" Claire felt her face turn from green to red. "My memory is patchy."

"Mine too, but I remember the songs *you* kept picking," he said, twisting slightly in his chair while clutching the back for support. "Even for me, there's only *so* many times I can *slam* it to the left if I'm having a good time and *shake* it to the right if I know that I feel fine. No, if *I'd* have been picking, it wouldn't have been the Spice Girls, dear."

"He does a mean Shirley Bassey," Marley whispered across the counter. "How about a salad?"

"Remember to tell my mother about this moment next time you see her because I'm going to say yes, and she'll never believe that I did."

"That's a promise."

"Better make it two," she said before Marley retreated to the kitchen. "No tomatoes on Damon's. He'll only pick them out."

While Marley made the salads at the back of the café, Claire leaned against the high breakfast bar along the side wall. The small television in the corner caught her eye.

"Is that the post office?" she whispered as she walked towards the morning edition of the local news. "They're in the square."

Claire turned up the volume as the camera panned to DI Ramsbottom. He stood to attention in front of the post office, awkwardly glancing down the camera lens as the presenter introduced him.

"Would you look at that *poor* man!" Eugene exclaimed. "If he pulls his toupee down any further, it will *fuse* with his eyebrows."

Someone in the café shushed Eugene, and Claire turned up the volume.

"That's correct," Ramsbottom said after a cough, his voice an octave deeper than usual. "The prints found on the gun did indeed belong to Tomek Kowalski, son of the late Eryk Kowalski shot here, at Northash Post Office, early on Saturday morning."

"And are the police *still* considering this a random burglary?"

"I'm afraid I can't comment on that, but I will say we are very keen to talk to Tomek as soon as possible."

"How long until you expect to have Tomek Kowalski in police custody?"

"Well, um…" Ramsbottom scratched at his golden hair as sweat dribbled down his face in stunning high-definition quality. "Tomek Kowalski's current location isn't known to the police, but we are using every resource afforded to us to track him down. If anyone has any information regarding his whereabouts, they should contact the police."

"And isn't it true that the police have already

interviewed him?" The reporter pushed the microphone closer to Ramsbottom's mouth. "How is your station reacting to letting a suspect slip through their fingers?"

"That's not what I said."

"And the rumours that your detective inspector role has been called into question in recent months?" The microphone moved closer. "Is that true?"

Ramsbottom slapped the microphone away.

"Who told you that?"

"A source."

"What source?"

"You don't deny it."

"You'll edit that out!" Ramsbottom warned with an extended finger. "I'm here to talk about the Eryk Kowalski case."

Ramsbottom's face turned increasingly red as he stared at the presenter. No one in the café let out a breath.

"We're live, Detective Inspector."

Ramsbottom looked awkwardly at the camera as more droplets trickled down his plump cheeks. He looked as though he was going to deliver a rebuttal, but he walked off-camera instead. The camera zoomed in on the DI as he scurried to his car, darting glances over his shoulder the whole way.

"Brace yourselves," Eugene announced excitedly. "I think Northash is about to go viral again, and not because of that woman with twenty-three cats in her council flat."

"Twenty-six," someone called out. "Molly had kittens."

Leaving the conversation to drift and bounce like it always did, Claire paid for her salads and left. In front of the post office, the camera crew were packing up while Ramsbottom talked on the phone in his car. She couldn't hear his conversation, but his flapping hands said enough.

At the candle shop, Damon practically had his nose pressed up against the glass.

"I think I was just on the telly," he said as she walked in.

"You weren't." She passed him a salad box. "Shop wasn't in frame."

"Then this sign was stupid." He screwed up a piece of paper and tossed it into the bin.

"What did it say?"

"'I'm on the telly.'"

"Genius."

"Why, thank you." Damon gave a slight bow before looking into the box. "*Salad*? What did I do wrong?"

"Temptation." She sank onto the stool behind the

counter and unfolded the cardboard box. "Why didn't you get me down off the pool table?"

"You seemed to be having fun," he said with a shrug. "And besides, I was up there too. We were two short, but we still made a decent Spice Girls between us. Even Sherlock needed a night off."

"Since you took the conversation in this direction," she mumbled through a mouthful, "Ramsbottom was just on the news talking about Tomek's prints being on the gun. If they find him, I think it might be over."

"Sounds like a closed case to me."

"I *knew* he was making Leo lie for him." She stabbed her fork into the leaves and vegetables; at least Marley had gone overboard with the dressing. "Poor guy was more on edge than normal."

"And your mum? Where does she fit into all of this now that the case is solved?"

"Still working on that." She tapped the side of her head. "Dad invited me to dinner tonight. We're going to sit her down and get it out of her. Lots of soft talking and open palms."

"We had to do something like that for my auntie when she went crazy on diet pills she bought off the internet," he said, taking the stool next to Claire. "Thin as a rake but as mad as a box of frogs. She would stay up for days at a time, brushing the carpet so all the strands lay in one direction."

"My mother's been doing similar," she said, "minus the diet pills." Claire stabbed her fork around some more. "Yesterday at the party, I saw her sneak off to…"

The air shifted outside. Police officers appeared from nowhere, all running towards The Hesketh Arms. One by one, they hurried down the path to the canal that Claire had taken. They headed across the bridge and into the forest on the other side. The camera crew stopped packing and caught up.

"What's going on?" Damon spat his mouthful of leaves into the bin. "Not sure how much more drama I can handle this week."

"I'm not sure," she replied, opening her laptop. "Might as well find out the same way everyone else does."

After a few clicks, she had on the same news channel as the café. Switching her gaze between the window and laptop, Claire worked through the salad. The segment was still in the studio.

"Quite nice, this."

"Is it?" Damon pushed his box away. "Think I'll wait for lunch."

Before Claire could defend the salad, the studio announced "a breaking development in the Northash

Post Office shooting case". They cut to the reporter, now hastily set up on the edge of the forest while police milled around behind him.

"There's been an extraordinary development right here in Northash." The presenter stepped slightly to the side to show a wall of officers blocking something. "Just behind me, a body has been discovered on a routine sweep of the same forest where the police found the gun used in the robbery. The police have yet to confirm the victim's identity; however, moments before we came back on the air, I overheard Detective Inspector Ramsbottom mention Tomek Kowalski. I must stress this has not been confirmed. Still, we have good reason to believe Tomek Kowalski's body has been found a stone's throw away from the scene where his father was murdered, days ago, with a gun containing Tomek's prints. A shocking twist in an unusual case."

Claire finished her salad and sighed as she slowly dabbed at the corners of her mouth.

"Well," she said as she shut the laptop. "It was never going to be that easy, was it?"

CHAPTER EIGHT

From the safety of the shop, Claire and Damon watched chaos unravel around the square. Shopkeepers and customers alike gravitated towards the canal until they could see nothing but the backs of heads. The police managed to push back the news crew, not that the camera ever left the cameraman's shoulder.

"What's going on?" Sally asked as she stepped into the empty shop in her formal workwear. "Feels like Saturday morning all over again."

"It is." Claire left the counter and observed the thickening madness through her window display. "They've found Tomek's body in the forest. According to the news, at least."

"Isn't he the guy Ramsbottom was talking about? Whose prints were on the gun?" Sally retrieved her phone from her handbag. "Have you seen the video? Everyone on my friends list has gone mad sharing it."

Claire almost said she'd witnessed the interview live on the telly, but the news clip on social media had been edited to within an inch of its life. The frame zoomed in on the sweat dribbling down DI Ramsbottom's red face. The old-fashioned noise of dial-up modem internet screeched in the background as Ramsbottom realised he was on live television. He walked off at double speed as music more suited to a circus played him out. Though the situation, as a whole, wasn't funny, Claire stifled a laugh at the antics of the fast-acting video editor.

"Haven't seen this much fuss since the woman with the twenty-three cats," Sally said as she put her phone away.

"It's twenty-six now," said Claire.

"Aw, did Molly have her kittens?" Damon asked as he walked around the counter. "What are you doing here, anyway? I thought you had a viewing in Christ Church Square?"

Claire narrowed her eyes on Damon. Since when did he know the details of Sally's daily schedule? Claire hadn't even known Sally was working so close today.

"Couldn't get into the property," said Sally as she gave one of the mango candles a sniff. "The chain's been drawn from inside, and I didn't have the back door key. It's probably that new girl who cries whenever you tell her she's done something wrong. I don't know when working with twenty-year-olds started feeling like babysitting ten-year-olds, but she's about on a level with my Ellie."

"I think that just means we're getting old," said Claire.

"Speaking of old, your birthday is coming up," Sally said, seemingly uninterested in the madness unfolding behind her. "One of the lads at work was talking about a new bar on Canal Street. Fire-breathing drag queens and cheap shots."

"Oh, no." Damon pressed his hand to his mouth and ran to the bathroom.

"Was it something I said?"

"He's tender after one too many pints last night." Claire pulled open the shop door. "Can you watch things until he gets back? I have a feeling it's about to be a quiet day."

"Where are you off to?"

"Two doors down while the police are distracted. I've had an idea."

"You're going to get a reputation for being nosey."

"In a village where everyone seems to know the goings-on of someone with twenty-six cats, I'll fit right in."

The crowd across the square had left the post office devoid of customers. Behind the counter, Leo was resting his head on his arms, but he shot up when Claire entered. The black eye had faded to a purple smudge, though he'd replaced his shiner with rings dark enough to announce he hadn't slept in days.

"Hi, Claire." He struggled to form a smile. "No chocolate today?"

"No," she said, glancing at the shelves she usually stuck to. "I'm here to see you. How are you doing, Leo?"

"Fine."

"I don't think that's quite true," she said, offering him a smile. "You worked with my mother for too long."

Claire attempted to laugh, but he only blinked slowly, his mind clearly somewhere else. Breaking his eye contact, the wall behind him caught Claire's attention. She hadn't noticed the change at first, but it was drastic.

Stationery had replaced the wall of alcohol.

"Had a change around?" she asked.

"Oh, I, um—"

"I saw the police here last night," she revealed before he scrambled for a lie. "Carrying out boxes of glass bottles, by the sound of it. It looked like a raid."

Leo fiddled with his glasses as his face darkened. He glanced back at the wall of stationery before nodding.

"Yeah," he said, his shoulders tensing up as he wrapped his arms around himself. "Turns out Eryk was buying fake alcohol. A girl's in the hospital from drinking too much of it." He paused before adding, "I only found out about it yesterday."

"I guess they took you in for questioning?"

She decided not to mention she'd seen him being ducked into a police car. Given how strange he'd been acting lately, she wanted to see if she could catch him out. He nodded again.

"I didn't have anything to tell them," he said with a tense shrug. "A few people complained here and there, but people complain about all sorts these days."

Claire wondered where – or even if – Eryk's supply preferences fit into the picture. Filing it away for later examination, she turned to why she'd come to the post office in the first place.

"Do you know what's going on out there?" she asked, noticing the black screen of the television in the corner. "The police are all over the square again."

Leo's eyes widened. "Why?"

"A body in the forest," she replied, watching for Leo's reaction. "They're saying it might be Tomek."

Leo's brows tightened low over his eyes as his focus vanished. From the slow blinks as he seemed to process the information, his surprise seemed genuine, at least to Claire.

Above them, the ceiling creaked as footsteps paced from one side to the other.

"My dad's upstairs sorting some stuff out," he explained, glancing upwards before looking at Claire. "Are you saying Tomek is dead?"

"It's looking that way. When did you last see him?"

"Two days ago," he said without missing a beat. "He didn't turn up for work."

"Didn't you call him?"

"I don't have his number," he said, staring down at a mobile phone atop a stack of the latest issue of Northash Observer. "We're not really friends."

"I got that impression." She chose her words carefully. "Did you hear about Tomek's prints turning up on the gun used in the burglary?"

"The police said something about it last night."

"You didn't mention Tomek holding the gun," she reminded him. "Was there a struggle with the gunman?"

"Yeah." He nodded quickly. "A struggle. I forgot."

"Seems like something you'd have remembered." She smiled again, but his surprise had shifted to suspicion. "Leo, was Tomek making you lie for him?"

"What are you getting at, Claire?" He snapped in a tone she'd never heard from him before. "It's been a crazy couple of weeks, okay?"

"Weeks?" She arched a brow. "It's only Wednesday, and the shooting was—"

The phone on the newspapers jumped to life, and the lit-up screen drew Claire's attention. Even upside down, she could clearly read the contact's name before Leo silenced the call and flipped the device.

Berna.

And there was a red heart next to her name.

"I'm shutting the post office," he said, walking around the counter and motioning to the door. "You're going to have to go."

"Leo, I just want—"

"Why should I care what you want, Claire?" he snapped, eyes filled with rage. "Please, just leave."

Leo frogmarched Claire to the door so quickly she didn't have time to register what was happening until she was on the pavement. The locks clicked behind her as a screen came down over the slightly frosted window in the door.

That wasn't like Leo.

That wasn't like Leo at all.

She pulled out her phone and scrolled through her recent contacts. Sally, Damon, Mum, Dad, Gran, Ryan. Only the latter had a heart next to their name.

Claire returned to her shop, expecting to see Sally and Damon – or at least one of them. A lone customer browsing the shelves offered Claire a tight smile, but no one was there to serve her.

All at once, Sally and Damon rushed out of the backroom.

"Right, I should get going," Sally announced, eyes fixed on her phone as she hurried to the door. "Showing some people around a place in Pendle, and they seem keen. See ya later."

Sally gave Claire a quick kiss on the cheek before she left. She smelled suspiciously like Damon's aftershave.

"I was born on a day," she whispered to Damon as she joined him behind the counter, "but it wasn't yesterday."

"I don't know what you mean."

"Sure, you don't."

Claire and Damon didn't talk much throughout the morning, content with their own thoughts. On the other side of the clock, the crowd swelled and shrank repeatedly.

Ramsbottom appeared infrequently, always in some sort of tizzy. Some of the 'Death Watchers' – a term Damon broke an hour-long silence to coin – passed through.

Unfortunately for Claire, the Death Watchers were also Candle Watchers. Some inhaled Claire's homemade creations, but most used the shop floor as their personal meeting ground to exchange gossip. They were no help in boosting the low sales Claire had seen since the shooting.

To make matters worse, she spotted Linda and Joan amongst the crowd early in the afternoon. She hadn't seen them since she'd overheard their gossip about her mother in the supermarket.

"Looking like suicide," Linda whispered to Joan as she half-heartedly poked around in a bowl of wax melts. "Poor lad was swinging from a tree."

Claire had been hearing similar rumours all morning.

"Guilt will do that," Joan replied.

"Did you see the video of that police fool online? Looked like he was going to burn his hair off with all that thinking."

"I've heard it's a wig."

"I *thought* it was too shiny."

"What was he even on the news for anyway? I missed that part."

"Dead lad's fingerprints were all over the gun that killed his father," Linda whispered as they moved onto the diffusers section. "Maybe Janet had nothing to do with it, after all. It looks like he killed his father and then killed himself."

"Have you seen her lately?"

"Not a peep, Joan. She's dodged the last two WI meetings. She's going doolally again, I swear. It's the 1993 church Nativity all over again. Remember when she lost her mind over losing that megaphone? Complete psycho. I don't know how poor Alan puts..."

Linda's voice trailed off as Claire stepped into their peripheral vision. She cleared her throat, and both women spun around, their polite smiles snapping into place like they had magnets pulling at the corners of their mouths from behind their ears.

"Ladies," she said, matching their smiles. "Please leave. You're barred."

"Excuse me?" Linda stiffened. "How dare—"

"How dare *you*," Claire cut in, remembering what Em had told her about a calm delivery helping others receive strong points. She inhaled and said, "You're supposed to be her friends."

FRESH LINEN FRAUD

"We are. It's just—"

"Too scandalous not to be discussed?" A lump rose in Claire's throat, but she fought it back; she wouldn't let them see her crack. "I know you all like to keep your smiles wide and your upper lips stiff, but my mum isn't well right now. More than ever, she needs a friend, and she's too proud to admit it."

"Well, I suppose we—"

"No." Claire shook her head. "Not you. She needs anyone but people like you right now. Don't you see that you're part of the problem?"

"You cheeky so-and-so!" Joan clutched her cardigan together. "No wonder you're not married, Claire Harris. Just you wait until your mother hears about this."

"I look forward to her grounding me," she said, stepping to the side and offering them the door. "Now, in case you didn't hear me, you're barred. You're not welcome here."

"We wouldn't come back anyway." Linda examined Claire from her feet to her hair. "Didn't smell a thing I liked. C'mon, Joan."

"And just so you know," she said before they reached the door. "My mother didn't lose that megaphone all those years ago. Ryan hid it. And in case you don't know who Ryan is, he's the hunky redhead who works at the gym, and he's my boyfriend. We might not be married, but he's worth a hundred of you. So, respectfully, you can stick your comments where the sun doesn't shine."

The two women left, deep in conversation as they scurried across the square. Despite the lava boiling in Claire's veins, she'd kept quiet enough that barely anyone had noticed the altercation – though she'd felt Damon's eyes on them the whole time.

"What was that about?"

"I might have just taken my stress out on two WI members," she said after a sip of water. "With the things they were just saying about my mum, they're lucky all I did was bar them."

"What things?"

"Let's just say if I'd overheard the same things five pints in last night, I might have tried to headbutt at least one of them." She perched on her stool. "Saying that, they've just reminded me why I wanted to look into what happened at the post office."

"It's not like anyone outside their little gang actually thinks your mother was involved."

"I know, but she's clearly in some trouble." She grabbed her jacket. "Are you okay to watch over things here?"

"Not like any of them are in a rush to buy."

"I'll be back before close."

"Where are you going?"

"Christ Church Square," she said, pulling on her jacket. "I want to find out what's going on in that house."

CHAPTER NINE

Ignoring the commotion, Claire walked through the village and wondered why the women had got to her so much. She knew her mother wasn't perfect, but they seemed to view her through a distorted funhouse mirror. They didn't know her at all, and yet they talked about her like they did.

That wasn't what upset Claire.

What upset her was the realisation that her mother had no friends.

No real friends.

Janet was always around people, usually women her own age, at fundraisers, fêtes, and functions. Still, she didn't have a Sally, a Damon, or an Em. She had no one to talk to about the things she wasn't comfortable talking about with her family.

Her mum was surrounded by acquaintances rooting for her downfall.

The notion punched Claire in the gut.

Christ Church Square, a smaller version of the main square minus the clock tower, backed onto the wall around Trinity Community Church's graveyard. There were benches, old-fashioned lampposts, a few parking spaces, and a row of terraced cottages on all sides.

Ryan's cottage sat in the middle of the main row, but Claire was only concerned with the house at the end.

From the outside, the end house looked abandoned. There were no lights beyond the window's newspaper coverings, and a Smith and Smith Estate Agents' sign jutted from the old stone.

"The chain," she whispered to herself, recalling Sally's missed viewing.

She stopped herself as she raised a hand to knock on the front door. While not as busy as the other square, people regularly passed through it with their prams and walking canes. She ventured around the back, taking her mother's route through the rear garden.

Like her mother had done, Claire gave the door a couple of confident knocks.

"Who is it?" a voice whispered through the door. "Janet?"

"Yep, it's me," she said, wincing at how little she sounded like her mother. "It's Janet."

The wooden door creaked open. A pale boy's face appeared in the dusty darkness, partially hidden behind chest-length dark blond hair. The one eye she could see opened wide, and Claire jammed her foot into the gap before he could slam the door.

"My name is Claire," she said quickly, wincing as the stranger attempted to close the door, foot and all. "I'm Janet's daughter. I'm sorry for lying. I only want to talk."

"Claire?" he replied, hidden behind the door. "The candle lady?"

"That's me."

He stopped hitting the door against Claire's foot and opened it, remaining hidden behind the back door. With no idea what she was about to find, Claire took one last breath and stepped into the haziness.

The kitchen was similar to Ryan's in size and layout only. Geometric wallpaper yellowed by time coupled with cupboards painted a bubbling green hinted that the place hadn't been redecorated since at least the 1970s.

The door closed behind her, drowning out most of

the light. One of her signature vanilla bean candle jars flickered amongst empty tins on a small dining table, almost burned down to the wick.

Hanging back by the door as though preparing to make a quick escape, the boy tucked his long hair behind his ears. A teenager for sure, but she couldn't quite place an age.

"Where's Janet?" he asked meekly, staring at the floor. "Did she send you?"

"No," Claire admitted, deciding honesty was the best policy. "She doesn't know I'm here. I saw her come here yesterday. I was at a party two doors down, and—"

"I heard the music," he said. "Janet brought me some cake."

"She did?" Claire smiled, sensing she wasn't in any danger. "Can I ask your name?"

"Ash."

"Nice to meet you, Ash," she said, stretching out a hand that he didn't take. "Do you like that candle?"

Ash looked back at the jar and nodded.

"Have I got Janet in trouble?"

"I'm not too sure," she said. "I was hoping you could tell me. She's been acting—"

A knock at the back door cut Claire off. She saw

the alarm bells ring behind Ash's eyes before he crept towards the back door.

"It's only me," Janet whispered. "Are you there, Ash?"

Ash opened the door, and Janet bustled in, staring into a white shopping bag.

"I bought more of those custard creams since you liked them so much, and some books. I know you didn't ask for them, but I imagine you're quite bored here on your—" Janet looked up from the bag, and her gaze immediately snapped onto Claire. "W-what are you doing here?"

"I saw you sneak over during the party."

"Ash, why don't you go grab another of those candles I brought you? This one is nearly done." Janet handed over the bag and sent Ash on his way. "That's a good boy."

"Mum, I—"

"What did you say to Ash?"

"Nothing," Claire said, pulling her arm from her mother's grip. "I was trying to get to the bottom of what's going on here."

"It's a long story," she replied, opening the back door. "I'm trying to do what's best by him, and that's all you need to—"

"I know about the pension fraud."

Janet gulped.

"How?"

"So, there is pension fraud?"

"You just said you know about it."

"I know it's why you were fired," Claire said, resting a hand on her mother's shoulder. "There's no need to keep lying. I know, and it's okay. You're going to be okay."

Janet's eyes misted over with tears, though none sprang free from her unblinking lashes.

"Janet?" the soft voice called down the stairs. "I'm down to the last candle."

"I'll fetch some more," she called back after sniffing hard to banish the tears. "I take it your father has invited you to my intervention tonight, so I'll explain then."

"Mum—"

"Please, Claire," Janet said, pushing her through the door. "I have everything under control."

For the second time that day, a door closed and locked behind Claire. Knowing she'd meet her mother's wrath if she dared to knock again, she left the house behind.

As she returned to the shop, she tried to piece

together what she'd just witnessed, but she could make neither heads nor tails of it. Once in the square, it didn't take long for something else to occupy her mind.

"Like I just told your officers, this is absurd!" exclaimed Duncan. He and DI Ramsbottom stood outside the post office. "It sounds like you're trying to arrest me."

"We just want to ask you some questions at the station," said Ramsbottom, gesturing towards the open door of the police car. "Two people connected to this post office have turned up dead in a single week."

"You've already confirmed my alibi!" he cried. "I was in Yorkshire on business when Eryk was shot."

"Are you currently the sole proprietor of Northash Post Office?" Ramsbottom asked. His sigh clearly indicated how thoroughly exhausted he was with the day.

"Well, technically—"

"Then I'm going to once again request that you come to the station." Ramsbottom glanced at two uniformed officers, both with their hands resting on their handcuffs. "I won't ask a third time, Mr Wilkinson."

Duncan and Ramsbottom stared off for an

uncomfortably long time, until the former conceded with a sigh. Jerking away when an officer attempted to guide him in by the head, Duncan ducked into the back seat of the police car on his own.

Ramsbottom jumped into the front seat, and they set off, only to immediately slam to a halt when a black car with tinted windows cut them off at the junction. The black vehicle rolled by slowly, apparently indifferent to the blaring police horn. When the black car finally turned, it circled the square and parked outside the pub, though no one emerged from behind its blacked-out windows.

Claire found her shop as busy as it had been when she left, though people were still shy of buying. For once, that suited her; she was far too distracted trying to make sense of what was going on.

"Everything circles back to the post office," she whispered to Damon. "What am I missing?"

"That we skipped lunch," he said, grabbing his wallet from under the counter, "and no, those salads definitely don't count. It's my turn to pull a vanishing act."

As the browsers idled around the shop, Claire's mind wrestled with the dots of information, trying to connect them.

She was confident about one thing.

Like the wick of Ash's vanilla candle, she was going to burn through the confusion to get to the bottom of this ever more complicated mess.

CHAPTER TEN

*N*eighbours twitched at their curtains as shouting filled the warm evening air in the cul-de-sac. Claire didn't need to wonder which of the large, detached houses the commotion was coming from; she recognised the voices.

"It's a funny world where I have nicer things to say about my daughter-in-law than her own mother!" Granny Greta roared from the sitting room as Claire quietly opened the front door. "You should be ashamed of yourself."

"*I* should be?" Moreen cried back. "How many of *my* children are in prison for murder?"

Claire winced as she kicked off her shoes. Of all the people to bring up Uncle Pat in an argument, of course it had to be Mean Moreen.

"You evil…" Greta's words trailed off, pain gnawing at the edges of her voice. "You keep Pat's name out of your bitter mouth."

"What are you going to do?"

"I'm so close to walloping you right now."

"Violence must run in the family."

"Keep this up, and I'll slap you so hard I send you back to whatever era supplies your hideous wardrobe!"

Still lingering by the door, Claire stifled a laugh. She heard her father sigh in the kitchen down the hall.

"Newsflash," Greta continued when Moreen didn't bite back. "They stopped requiring that hemlines graze the floor a century ago. You should know. *You* were there."

Not wanting to get dragged into the fray, Claire crept past the open door, only glancing in long enough to see her grandmothers planted on either side of the coffee table. Once in the kitchen, she pushed the door gently against the frame to close it.

"They've been at each other's throats for half an hour, little one," Alan revealed, accepting Claire's kiss on the cheek as he fried onions in a pan. "I've given up trying to separate them. Something tells me they're enjoying the drama."

"What caused it this time?"

"Greta wouldn't get out of Moreen's armchair," he

said through slightly pursed lips. "*My* armchair, not that I've been able to sit in it since she arrived."

"Is Mum hiding in the downstairs bathroom again?"

"Garden," he said, adding chopped garlic to the pan. "At least, I assume that's where she is. If she's climbed over the fence and escaped through Ian's farm, I wouldn't blame her."

Leaving her father to turn up his mud-caked portable radio, Claire exited through the back door. She scanned the pristine garden, but there was no sign of her mother. On the hill beyond the farm, the Warton Candle Factory stood proudly against the bleeding sunset. She didn't spot her mother running around the fields either. At the bottom of the garden, the door to her father's beloved potting shed was slightly ajar.

"Is that you, Alan?" Janet asked softly as Claire pushed open the door. "I'll be back in a minute."

Claire entered the shed, expecting to see her mother standing uncomfortably, surrounded by the dust, mud, and cobwebs. She wasn't, nor was she at the potting desk. Of all places, Janet balanced on the small, upturned terracotta plant pot in the corner that had remained unmoved since Claire's childhood. Anyone else would have been ordered off, but Claire took pity and sat in the recycled office chair.

To her surprise, her mother didn't stiffen her spine, stuff her tissue up her cardigan sleeve, or force a smile. Hunched in the corner with her elbows resting on her knees, she continued to dab at her eyes.

"Are they still at it?"

"Like their lives depend on it."

"I can usually handle one at a time," she said with a dry laugh, "but not both at once. I had to get out of there. I thought I'd see what all the fuss was about with this shed. It's quiet down here."

"Have you been converted?"

"Don't get ahead of yourself, dear," she said, drying her eyes before straightening a little and looking around the place. "I can't tell if it needs a bottle of bleach or blowing up." She smiled wanly. "Since you've found out so much behind my back, I suppose I should tell you what's been going on."

"You didn't leave me much choice," said Claire. "You shut down. We're worried."

"Yes, yes, point taken." Janet exhaled. "I was raised to not talk about things as trivial as feelings. It's hard to break the habits of a lifetime, dear. I don't even know where to start."

"Start with Ash."

"Ash." Her lips pricked up. "All my years in this world, and I don't think I've ever met such a sweet, sensitive soul as that child. He'd come to the post office with Elsie and wouldn't say a word. He always hid behind her."

"How old is he?"

"Fourteen," she said. "I heard about Elsie's passing and didn't give him a second thought. I didn't even know his name. I didn't even know he was a boy until he came to the post office alone and I heard him speak for the first time. Long hair will do that. I offered to cut it, but he didn't take me up on it."

Claire thought about the night before her fourteenth birthday. Her mother had forced her into a chair in the kitchen to give her hair 'a little trim' that left her with a one-inch fringe that wouldn't lie flat. The hairdresser they rushed to straightaway blamed Janet's too-firm tension and suggested a hat.

"Probably for the best," said Claire. "So, Ash came into the post office?"

"He could barely speak above a whisper," she said. "He was trying to cash his grandmother's pension. I knew she'd died, and even if she hadn't, he was too young. He didn't put up a fight when I said I couldn't do that. He just said 'oh' and left. I didn't think much of it, but then I saw him two days later as I left the church after a WI meeting. He was sneaking around the back of Elsie's house. I knew she lived there alone. I was going to give him hell for trying to break in, but I realised he was squatting. Eryk fired me because of what I did next."

"You cashed Elsie's pension for Ash?"

Janet nodded solemnly.

"I knew I was breaking some law," she said, "but I did it anyway. The government usually stop it from being drawn after a death, but the system let me, so I drew her pension and took it to him. It's only £134.25 a week. Hardly enough for most people to live on, but it was enough for Ash. He had nothing. He has no one."

"No other family?"

"A father," she said, snarling slightly. "Nasty piece of work, from what Ash told me. When Ash came out to his dad, he kicked him out. I don't know what he came out as, so don't ask. One of my magazines said it's not politically correct to ask these days unless they offer it up, not that it matters. He's just a child. A scared child, living in his dead grandmother's house, waiting for the world to fall down around him."

"Oh, Mum." Claire reached out and clutched her hand. "Didn't you think to call social services?"

"That was my *first* thought, Claire," she said quickly. "The second I suggested it, he broke down. I've never seen anything like it. Crying, begging, pleading. They put him into care before his grandmother took him in, and he said he couldn't go back. I've been trying to talk him around, but he's adamant he's staying where he is."

"He can't."

"I know that," Janet said, "and on some level, he must know it too. He doesn't see any options ahead of him. He's so scared of the world. I didn't know what else to do, so I've been taking care of him. Bringing him food and magazines, although he likes my magazines about as much as you do."

"And the pension?"

"Twice more," she said, looking down at the floor. "The final time was the night before my party. Someone from the council finally noticed and called Eryk. He came straight to the house, and, well, you know the rest."

"He could have waited until morning."

"I thought that at the time," she said with a shrug, "but I'm lucky he didn't go straight to the police. I've committed fraud, Claire. I didn't even realise it was fraud until Eryk said the word."

"Because you were doing it with the best intentions."

"And, after forty years of service, I've disgraced myself in the process." She frowned as her eyes misted over. "That's not all Eryk said. Felt like he'd been bottling up his feelings towards me for years, and he didn't hold back. He called me cruel and callous. Apparently, I'm a nightmare to work with and people are scared of me."

"Oh, Mum, he was just trying to—"

"Upset me?" she interrupted. "I know that's what he wanted, and he succeeded. And not because of when he said it, why he said it, or even what he said. I've been so upset because he was right. It's true. I've seen myself be those things for so many years, never able to rein myself in. I don't mean to come across that way, but I do. I'm no fool, Claire."

"There's more to you than that."

"But they don't cancel each other out," she said, applying the tissue to her eyes again. "I always wanted to be different from my mother, but I became her. It's never been more evident than it is now, having her in the house. Maybe that's just how the cards fall."

"If that was the case, I'd become you, and I don't see that happening anytime soon." Claire ducked to meet her mother's downward gaze. "And you're nothing like your mother. She's had an influence on you, but you are so much more; you have a whole other side. The Harris side. Do you think Grandmother Moreen would do what you did for Ash?"

"Commit fraud?"

"*Care.*" Claire squeezed her mum's hand. "Even if she'd got as far as finding Ash at Elsie's, do you think she'd have gone out of her way to help?"

"Well, no."

"And would she be upset knowing people saw her as cruel?" Claire asked. "I doubt it. In fact, I think she'd enjoy it. You don't."

"I ... suppose."

"She doesn't even possess the self-awareness to question herself like you are now. Do my fresh linen candles smell the same as my mango candles?"

Janet blinked. "No, but what does that have to do with the price of bread?"

"They share one of the same citrus notes, but they're still vastly different." She squeezed harder. "Your mother raised you. Her scent is on you. For better or worse, you can't escape the parts of yourself that remind you of her."

"Then what's the point?"

"Do you *want* to be like that?"

"No, but—"

"That's the point," Claire said, releasing her mum's hand. "You're in here reflecting, and she's in there bringing up Uncle Pat to upset Granny Greta."

"Oh, she didn't?"

"She did."

"That woman." Janet pinched between her brows. "You know, it surprised me how quickly Greta jumped to my defence when my mother started on me."

"I thought it erupted over an armchair?"

"Oh, it did. Apparently, I should have foreseen the need for two identical armchairs when I redecorated the living room for just such an occasion." She rolled her eyes. "Greta told her she was talking nonsense. Those weren't her exact words, but I won't repeat them. I didn't stick around for much longer."

"Can't hide at the bottom of the garden forever. Isn't that what you always tell me and Dad?" Claire pushed herself up. "Should we see if they've drawn blood?"

"If we must."

Back in the kitchen, Claire's joke about drawing blood seemed like clairvoyance. Blue lights flashed through the windows down the hallway while the mince in the frying pan sizzled, abandoned, and the radio blared.

"I've been waiting for them to come for me," Janet worried, hurrying to the oven to turn off the hob. "It was only a matter of time before they discovered my fraud."

"Wait here," Claire said, pulling the kitchen door shut as she went.

She hurried past the empty sitting room and through the front door. A lone police car was parked in the middle of the cul-de-sac while two officers spoke with Greta and Alan. Around the perimeter, the curtains continued twitching.

Claire hung back, content that her father's smile as he spoke with the officers meant they weren't here to haul away her mother. Eventually, they climbed in the car and drove away.

"Go on!" Greta called around the cul-de-sac, "Get a good look! The show's over, folks."

The curtains dropped as Greta and Alan approached Claire, both looking exhausted, though she guessed their reasons were different.

"One of the neighbours called the police," Alan explained as he hobbled back into the house with Claire's help. "Not that I'm surprised, given the way they were carrying on."

"I said nothing I regret," Greta said with a firm nod. "She's gone and locked herself up in the bedroom. She can give it, but she clearly can't take it."

They followed Greta down to the kitchen, where Janet was scraping the beef and onion mince mixture from the burned pan into the bin.

"Takeaway it is," Claire announced with a clap, already diverting to the drawer full of menus. "Any preferences?"

"I'd prefer a drink," Greta said, propping herself up at the sideboard. She poured herself a glass of whisky and took a sip. "Oh, crikey. Still this same stuff? Alan, where did you get this muck? Drinking a bottle of nail varnish remover would be more pleasant."

"It's the usual stuff from the post office."

"Post office?" Claire's ears pricked up. "Gran, don't drink that. It might not be real whisky."

"How can whisky not be real whisky?" she asked, examining the bottle. "What's fake whisky when it's at home?"

"You might not have been far off with the nail varnish comment." Alan took the bottle from his mother and sniffed at the opening. "A few years ago, we busted an operation not too far from here for bottling and selling knock-off alcohol. A man and a woman died before we found them."

"Died?" Greta cried.

"You only had a sip," he reminded her. "But they use anything they can get their hands on and colour it to look like anything they want. Little one, what made you say that?"

"Because there was a raid at the post office a few

days ago." Claire joined her mother, already scrubbing the burned pan, in the kitchen. "You said it yourself, Mum. Dodgy alcohol and cigarettes."

"Only based on what customers have been complaining about lately," she said, squirting in more washing up liquid. "I stayed out of it. Ordering wasn't my job. We kept the shop and post office sides of things separate."

Claire opened the cupboard containing the bins. Perfectly designed for their needs, there were separate bins for general waste, plastic, cardboard, and glass. She pulled off the lid to the glass bin, glad to see it hadn't been emptied. The bottles clanked together until she found what she was looking for.

"They look the same," Claire said as she compared the newer bottle with the older one. "Except there. Look."

Claire rolled the two bottles under the light. One label's quality seal had metallic markings, and the other's was dull and flat.

"A woman is in hospital," she said. "Do you think this could be connected to Eryk's death?"

"I thought Tomek did it?" Janet asked as she put the pan on the straining board. "Him killing himself like that should make it an open and shut case, no?"

"That's what you'd think," said Alan, his fingers

drumming on the counter. "I know the officers they sent tonight from my days at the station. They were more than happy to oblige when I asked if they had any updates."

"Non-public updates," Greta pointed out.

"It's not confirmed," he said, lowering his voice, "but there are whispers that Tomek's death isn't as simple as it seems. They haven't ruled it as a suicide yet, which means they're exploring options."

"And what reason would Tomek have for killing his father?" Greta asked as she poured gin into a new glass.

"To run the post office?" Janet suggested. "When I spoke with Leo on Monday, he knew nothing of my firing. On Tuesday, I foolishly thought I could turn up for work and nobody would know because Eryk hadn't had the chance to set it in stone. Tomek made it very clear *my* job was now *his*, and I wasn't welcome."

Alan limped into the kitchen and kissed Janet on the cheek. Claire wondered if this was the first time she'd admitted to her firing out loud – in the house, anyway.

"But why kill himself?" Claire asked. "Would Tomek even inherit his father's share of the post office? Surely it would go to his wife. Or even Duncan?"

"What if Tomek killed Eryk, and someone else killed Tomek?" Greta mused, dropping into a seat at the dining table. "I don't know. Something to think about."

And think about it, Claire did. Over a Chinese food banquet (which Moreen didn't emerge to partake of), the conversation drifted, but Claire's mind played that one thought on a loop.

Leaving the cul-de-sac in a calmer state than she'd found it, Claire walked Granny Greta home. On her way to her own flat, she stopped outside the dark post office, desperately wishing she knew what had really happened in there on Saturday morning.

Two of the witnesses were dead.

But one was still alive.

She just needed to get Leo to talk.

CHAPTER ELEVEN

*A*t quarter to noon the next day, the summer sun finally broke through the veil of clouds after a morning of light showers.

Seizing the opportunity to remain dry, Claire hauled the box she'd spent all morning curating to Christ Church Square. As with her previous visit, she walked to the back of Ash's house, where she placed the box on the kitchen doorstep.

Knowing her mother, Ash likely had a stock of tinned food, so Claire had opted for the 'junk' that wouldn't cross Janet's mind to provide: crisps, biscuits, chocolate, ketchup, and pop – as well as a fresh supply of candle jars.

The box wouldn't fix the situation, but as Damon

had pointed out, there was no reason she couldn't try to put a smile on Ash's face.

Instead of knocking, she slipped a 'From Claire x' note through the gap under the door and left.

During the quiet spell of rain, she'd gone in circles researching the unique situation. The internet bounced her from squatter's rights to the legality of a teenager living alone to Janet's culpability in enabling the situation.

All roads led to the same conclusion.

Alert social services.

Claire had gone as far as typing the number into her phone, but she couldn't bring herself to press the call button thanks to her mother's words.

"The second I suggested it," Janet had said in the shed, "he broke down."

It was the right thing to do.

The responsible thing to do.

But what Ash needed and wanted didn't align. As Damon had pointed out, what Ash needed *legally* might not be the best thing for him as a person.

Claire understood her mother's conflict, but the current situation couldn't continue. She just didn't know what the solution might be.

Back in the square, the gym pulled Claire's attention away from Ash's dilemma as the doors burst open and Anna Kowalski charged out in floods of tears. Em followed right behind, her calls going unheeded.

Behind the wheel of a car parked further down the street, Berna used the pull-down mirror to apply mascara while the radio played. She glanced at Claire through the rolled down window as she approached. She averted her gaze to the rear-view mirror to watch her mother march towards the car.

The yoga class friendliness had gone, but Claire could tell Berna had recognised her. Claire drew nearer and opened her mouth to offer condolences on her brother's death. The window slid up, as did the volume of the radio.

The glare of the window where Berna's face had been reflected Claire's shock. Still sobbing, Anna collapsed into the passenger seat, and Berna wasted no time starting the engine. She sped around the square, turning up Park Lane.

"That's not how that should have gone," said Em as Claire joined her in front of the busy gym. "I fear I may have put my foot in it."

Claire spotted Ryan through the glass doors. He was training someone on the treadmill, but he wasn't grinning as he'd been on her previous visit. Perhaps he saved that for when Claire was in?

"Knowing you, Em, I doubt you put your foot in it intentionally."

"What does intention matter when such upset is the result?" Em inhaled, closing her eyes as she tilted her face up to the sun. "Anna sought my spiritual guidance, but there was little I could say to ease her pain. She's booked a one-way ticket back to Poland for tomorrow. I shouldn't have suggested that such an action might plausibly be perceived as guilt."

"You're not wrong," Claire said with a shrug. "The phone calls, the life insurance, the plane ticket. It paints a picture."

"And today wasn't the day to show her such a picture," she said, looking at the path next to The Hesketh still blocked by police. "The words fighting on the tip of your tongue are perhaps the last things someone in distress needs to hear. To lose a husband and son in the same week is a loss more devastating than anyone can comprehend until they've experienced it. Compassion and empathy are hands that can only reach so far."

"What about funerals?" Claire asked. "Surely she'd want to stay for those?"

"She wants to fly them to Poland," Em revealed. "The police have released Eryk's body but not

Tomek's. They ruled on a cause of death this morning. Strangulation."

"Oh," Claire said, surprised. "I heard it might not be suicide."

"Strangulation at the hand of a fellow human being," Em clarified, shaking her head. "Tomek was already dead when the noose was tightened."

Lost for words, Claire stared at what she could see of the forest behind the pub. The theory that the guilt of committing his father's murder drove Tomek to take his own life disintegrated. A dozen new questions fought for her consideration.

"He must have known something," Claire mused, eyes still on the trees as new grey clouds moved in behind them. "Or someone killed him as revenge for killing Eryk?"

"Whatever the explanation, the police are intent on interviewing Anna and Berna as often as they can," she whispered. "Anna is certain they're trying to build a case around her, which is why fleeing the country right now is the worst thing she can do."

"It'll cause an INTERPOL witch hunt if they have even a sliver of evidence against her."

"I hope she comes to her senses before the flight," Em said, turning away from the sun. "And if she doesn't, maybe there's a—"

"A chance she's guilty?"

Em nodded solemnly. "The conversation you heard that suggested she might have a lover other than Eryk?" Em exhaled. "It wasn't a direct admittance, but she said she had bought two tickets. I asked if one was for Berna, and she said she'd given up trying to get her to go. She said she'd probably go alone if 'he doesn't answer her calls'. Who 'he' is, I don't know."

"Strange."

"Yet not the strangest thing she said." Em moved in closer and looked around the square. "She thinks she's being tracked and followed."

"By the police?"

"By men in black cars." Em pulled open the gym door. "Given everything that's happening in her life right now, I fear she may be on the edge of losing herself."

Claire didn't follow Em into the gym.

A shiny black car was parked between two police cars in front of the pub.

No registration plate.

Blacked-out windows.

Exactly like the car that cut off the police as they took in Duncan for questioning.

Feeling silly for playing into the paranoia, Claire walked up to the car. Only the faintest silhouettes were visible in the front seats. She knocked on the driver's window, expecting the people inside to roll down the glass and laugh off the suggestion that their activity was anything untoward.

The window didn't budge.

Engine gurgling to life, the car pulled away from the kerb and drove slowly around the square. It crawled to a near stop outside the closed post office before turning up Park Lane, just as Berna and Anna had done.

"Fancy seeing you here," Ryan said as he approached from the direction of the gym. "Staring at anything interesting?"

"A black car," she said, turning to face him but unable to take her eyes from Park Lane. "Anna thinks she's being followed."

"Grief does strange things to people."

She opened her mouth to mention that it wasn't the first time she'd noticed a similar car in the square, but she thought better of it; maybe she was as paranoid as Anna.

"I'm off for half an hour if you want to grab something to eat?" he asked.

"I'd love that."

Claire attempted to push everything other than spending time with Ryan to the back of her mind. It only lasted as long as it took them to queue up for two portions of salt-and-vinegar-drenched chips at The Abbey Fryer fish and chip shop.

As they picked at their chips and headed towards Starfall Park, Claire couldn't contain herself. When they reached the Chinese rock garden, she told Ryan all about her mother's fraud and the dilemma with Ash.

"And here I was saying he was Elsie's granddaughter," Ryan said as they sat on the stone seating circle under the pointed, Asian-inspired pergola. "I'll keep an eye on the house. He's only a few years older than Amelia."

"At least it gets my mum out of the picture with the post office." She dragged one of her last chips through the salt at the bottom of the paper. "Not that I know what the picture is. Someone's lying about something, and I'm only catching glimpses."

"I didn't realise you were so invested."

"It's bugging me," she said. "An apparently random shooting followed by a faked suicide in the same week? And the victims are father and son?" She grimaced. "I don't suppose you know where Leo Wilkinson lives?"

Ryan shook his head.

"I really need to talk to him," she said, staring off into the distance. "I hoped I'd get the chance this morning, but the post office never opened. He's right in the middle of the business and the family."

"Oh."

"I might have the wrong end of the stick, but there's a chance Berna is pregnant with Leo's baby," she explained. "He could be covering for her? Eryk was trying to send Berna out of the country. Maybe she turned up and shot him to stop it? But why Tomek? I gather there wasn't any love lost between them, but why?"

"I'm not sure."

"And what about Anna? She's in a rush to leave. From the sounds of it, her marriage wasn't bursting with happiness. She could have killed Eryk ... but surely not her son?"

"Right."

"And where does Duncan fit into it?" she wondered, almost to herself. "The police must have released him. His alibi of being in Yorkshire when Eryk died probably held up. If they'd charged him with something, we would have heard about it."

"Yeah."

"Which is why I need to speak to Leo. He's the key. He *has* to be. I wonder if my Mum has his phone number or knows…"

Claire's sentence trailed off as she averted her gaze

from the factory's chimney on the hill. Like Claire, Ryan stared off into the distance, though he didn't appear to be focused on anything.

"Am I boring you?" She playfully nudged his arm. "My mum thinks she has too much of her mother in her, but I know I definitely have too much of my dad in me."

"No, it's fine." He blinked, snapping back to the moment. "It's not you."

Claire's stomach knotted. So consumed with questions and theories, she hadn't bothered to ask how Ryan was doing. Now that she was properly looking at him, it was obvious something was off.

"Talk to me," she said softly, rubbing his freckled shoulder with her thumb. "I'm here."

Ryan pulled a small white envelope from his shorts pocket and handed it to Claire. He didn't look at it. The address belonged to the bed and breakfast Ryan had lived in when he first moved back to Northash, but Amelia's name occupied the first row.

Already suspecting what she'd find, Claire pulled out a small card with a bland floral design.

The contents were written in Spanish.

The knot tightened.

The final word needed no translation.

Mamá.

"Fergus chased me down this morning to give me this," he explained. "I gave everyone in her family the B&B's address when we first arrived. I thought it would tempt her to come out of hiding." He took the card from Claire and read, "'To my darling Amelia. I miss you very much. Happy birthday. From Mother.'"

Claire scrambled for something to say, but the knots spread from her stomach to her throat. She'd never met or spoken to Maya, though she remembered the pictures Ryan had shown her all those years ago. Most people went on lads' holidays with their college friends to do anything except find a relationship, but not Ryan. He returned with a sunburn and declarations of love for a Spanish beauty.

"Can you believe it?" he asked. "She ran off with the only mate I made over there and turned her back on us. I've spent all year trying to contact her for the sake of our children, and she's dodged me at every turn. And then this shows up. No apology, no explanation, not even an age on the front. Not that it's even a birthday card."

Elbows resting on his knees, Ryan dug his fingers into his red hair. Maya's first contact had been inevitable, but Claire hadn't expected it to be like this.

"How did Amelia react?"

"I haven't shown her." He looked at her through the gap under his arm. "You don't think I should, do you?"

"Doesn't she have a right to see it?"

"Things have finally settled." He sat up straight. "It's taken months to get the kids used to their new life. They're happy. I can't ruin that now. I won't."

"But wouldn't Amelia *want* to see it?" she asked calmly. "To know her mother is thinking about her?"

"It's three sentences, Claire." Standing up, he held out the card. "It will just reignite the false hope that their mother is just going to show up and everything will be alright again. Maya chose to leave."

"But what if she does show up one day?"

"Then she can explain where she's been to her daughter's face." Shaking his head, he said, "Honestly, Claire, I thought you'd get where I was coming from."

"I do." She stood and took his hands. "But—"

"But you still think I should show her?" He tugged his hands away. "Dangle that carrot in front of my daughter? You know how hard it's been."

"If I were Amelia, I'd want to know."

"But you've never been Amelia," he said, taking a step back. "You don't know what it feels like to sit by a window waiting for someone who'll never show up. Your parents are still together. You don't understand what three sentences like this can do to a child."

"I—"

"I need to get back to work," he said, barely able to look at her. "I-I'll see you later."

Ryan stalked off into the rain without so much as a kiss on the cheek.

Claire sank into her seat, watching the rain fall and trying not to dwell on the nagging thought that she might have witnessed the end of their relationship before it even had a chance to start.

CHAPTER TWELVE

*C*laire spent the rest of the workday on autopilot.

When it was busy, she laughed at customers' jokes, made small talk, and gave recommendations with ease.

In the lulls, she asked Damon about his latest *Dawn Ship 2* strategies, and he obliged with unceasing explanations. She only had to nod and make the right noises. If he stopped, a vague question would send him down another fifteen-minute rabbit hole.

She never understood, but she always listened.

Not today.

Somehow, she got to closing without Damon noticing that anything was off. She declined his offer of a drink and locked the front door behind him. In the window's reflection, her smile was convincing.

163

Claire had always wondered how most people couldn't see through her mother's 'everything is fine' expression.

Now, she understood.

She hadn't *wanted* to talk about her feelings.

She hadn't *wanted* to acknowledge them.

So, she smiled.

She smiled, and nobody noticed.

Once the lights were off, she went up to her flat. Domino and Sid greeted her, ready for their evening meal. After feeding them, she sank into a bubble bath, hoping it would help her to relax her mind.

It didn't work.

The silence only drove her crazier.

While a lasagne for one spun around in the microwave, she turned on the TV. She flicked through the high-numbered radio stations until something loud and thumping caught her ear.

She was too restless to sit.

She straightened the magazines and books on the coffee table. She stuffed as much of her overflowing laundry basket into the washing machine as would fit. Picking at her lasagne, she attacked the mountain of plates in the sink.

And then the rest of the kitchen.

And sitting room.

And bathroom.

And guest bedroom.

And master bedroom.

Claire didn't notice the clock tower outside strike midnight. She didn't see Domino chewing up one of her bras under the bed. She didn't notice anything until she was sorting her clothes and found the shoebox at the back of her wardrobe.

Leaning against the cold radiator, she peeled off the tatty lid held together by tape. She flipped it:

To Claire,

It's easy to forget all the good times we've had, so I thought I'd remind you.

Happy Eighteenth Birthday!

Your best friend, Ryan

PS: We're getting old.

Glossy photographs from their childhood and teenage years taken with various disposable cameras filled the box to the brim. Snapshots of birthday parties, school plays, concerts, her mother's annual BBQs, and everything in between.

"That boy is like your shadow!" her mother always said. "You need other friends."

Claire had Sally, too, but not like she had Ryan. They grew up side-by-side in the cul-de-sac, sharing almost every moment of their lives. She only had enough photographs with one person to fill a shoebox.

Flicking through the memories, she came across her and Ryan perched on the stairs in her mother's house a dozen redecorations ago. Claire straightened her thin, mousy hair, longer than it had any right being, to within an inch of its life. Ryan had so much gel in his hair that it almost looked brown, and his arm was around her shoulders.

"Closer," Sally had instructed when taking the

picture. "Why don't you give her a birthday kiss, Ryan?"

The occasion had been Claire's sixteenth birthday party. The one time, after much persuasion from her father, her mother had allowed her to have a birthday party with no adults. No alcohol, either – not that they'd listened. Back then, all it took was a can of cider.

"I'm going to tell him," she'd slurred to Sally in the garden while her beloved *Saints & Sinners* album by All Saints blared inside. "I'm going to tell Ryan I love him tonight."

"Finally, mate!"

She never did.

She'd be thirty-six before the end of the month.

Twenty years later, and she still hadn't told him. Maybe she'd already missed her last chance?

The sound of smashing glass floated through the open bedroom door. A photograph in her hand, she walked through the kitchen, expecting to see Domino knocking one of her drying glasses off the straining board. She wasn't. She was chewing up Claire's second favourite bra under the coffee table.

More smashing drifted through the front window, opened after spraying too much bleach when scrubbing the bathroom.

Was someone destroying her shop?

Claire sprinted downstairs, but the window was where she'd left it. She carefully unlocked the door and popped her head out. Yet again, the few people still in the dark square had their gazes trained on the post office.

"You *ruined* my life!" Anna screamed as she busted another of the window panels with a golf club. "I hate you! I *hate* you!"

Claire's instincts sent her running towards Anna to calm her, but the club's swing in her direction shut her instincts up. Safely back in her shop, she called the local station.

As Anna, raging, continued destroying the front of the post office, Claire perched on the stool behind her shop's counter. In the dark, she looked down at the photograph in her hand and laughed.

It showed another birthday party, this time her fourteenth. Clutching the yellow Tamagotchi her dad had bought her, she blew out her candles from under a giant hat. Claire would have preferred to wear Uncle Pat's flat cap, but it didn't disguise her one-inch fringe as well as her mother's pink-plumed wedding hat did.

Over one shoulder, Sally's pursed lips blew out half the candles. Like he'd been in all the other pictures,

Ryan was glued to Claire's side, the only sad face in a sea of happiness.

Claire stroked the troubled smile in the picture, remembering what had caused the pained expression. The day before, his excitement had been uncontainable thanks to his dad calling for the first time in two years.

"I invited him to your party." Ryan had beamed over the garden fence that night. "Is that okay?"

Claire had been as excited as Ryan. It was all they talked about all morning. By the time she was ready to blow out the candles, most of the party had been over, and the boy in the picture had lost hope that his father was going to show up.

Ryan had been right in the park.

She didn't understand what that felt like.

No wonder he didn't want to show Amelia the card.

As the police snapped Anna into handcuffs, Claire returned to her unusually pristine flat. Flicking through more of the pictures, she allowed the one thought she'd been avoiding all night to run riot in her brain.

It wasn't so much the disagreement she was trying to avoid, it was the reason behind it.

The card.

The baggage.

Maya.

Unlike the box bursting with memories, Claire didn't have Ryan to herself anymore. Maya had reached out, and it was just a matter of time before she showed her face.

After seventeen years apart, Claire wasn't sure she could lose Ryan a second time.

CHAPTER THIRTEEN

"*A*re you sure you're not insecure, mate?" Sally asked, pressing her hand down on Claire's head. "Hold still! One good stretch, and I'll be able to touch it."

"Stretch then, because I *will* drop you," Claire ordered, swaying as she clung to Sally's thighs around her neck. "And of course I'm insecure. I've never done any of this adult relationship stuff."

Sitting on Claire's shoulders, Sally let go of Claire's head and took an unbalancing swipe at the ceiling. Claire attempted to lock her buckling knees in place, but even if she wasn't the one trying to balance on someone else's shoulders, she was far from a gymnast.

"It *is* damp," Sally said, holding onto Claire's head

with both hands as they wobbled around the empty room. "I *knew* it."

Claire let out a relieved breath as Sally slid down her back. In the middle of the master bedroom, they stared up at the faint mark on the ceiling.

"That little liar," Sally whispered, looking through the open doorway. "Paint discoloration my backside. I know damp when I see it."

"Then why did you insist on sitting on my shoulders to check?"

"I know damp when I *touch* it, then." Sally elbowed her in the ribs. "Have you spoken to Ryan today?"

Claire shook her head. "I haven't seen him since he walked off in the park yesterday," she said, looking out of the window at the lingering clouds in the distance. "I can't tell if we're intentionally avoiding each other or if it's just one of those days where we're both busy."

"Ask him?"

"If he's avoiding me?"

"Why not?" Sally shrugged, running her hands down a crack in the plaster next to the window frame. "Paul was always so passive-aggressive, I got into the habit of confronting him. Worked out great." She winked over her shoulder. "Actually, I might not be the best person to take relationship advice from. But Ryan's not like that. He's probably embarrassed and doesn't know what to say. Test the waters with a text."

"Or he's realised it's not working?" Claire patted down her pockets. "What should I say?"

"Keep it light. Send him that Boris Johnson in the Berlin bar joke."

"He's the one who sent it to me." She dug her hands in her pockets. "I think I've left my phone in your car."

"Do you really think it's not working?" Sally arched a brow as they left the master bedroom. "You've only been seeing him for a month."

"Maybe," she said with a shrug. "The fact he hasn't even *kissed* me can't be a good sign."

"Forget him for a second. Do *you* think it's working? Do *you* enjoy being with him?"

"More than anyone."

"Cheers." Sally ribbed her again. "But I'll take it. That's all that matters. He tries to spend all his free time with you. He's just taking time to warm up to the situation. His kids aren't the only ones adjusting."

They walked down the creaky, uncarpeted staircase and found the estate agent on his phone in the kitchen. He switched on his customer service smile when he noticed them.

"So?" he asked hopefully. "Right in your price range, four bedrooms, lovely garden. Do you like?"

"Ticks all the boxes." Sally nodded, taking in the kitchen. "Not for me, though."

"Oh," the estate agent's hopeful smile soured, though he tried his best to keep the remnants on his face. "No problem. Let me know if you want to view any others."

Claire followed Sally out of the house and through the front garden. She looked back at the large, detached house, wondering if her lack of experience had made her miss something.

"I thought it was perfect," she said, glancing at Sally out of the corner of her eye. "You were nit-picking before we walked through the front door. And don't tell me it's because it's your job. That only means you know how easy it is to fix those tiny problems."

"Didn't feel right."

"Have any of them?"

"The next one might."

"Now who's avoiding the questions?" It was Claire's turn to elbow Sally in the side. "Is this about the house you're in now?"

"I told you, I want to leave."

"Wanting to and being ready to aren't the same thing."

"That Em is rubbing off on you." Sally opened her handbag and pulled out her car keys. "But maybe.

Once Paul was out of the picture, I thought I was ready to get out of there."

"But?"

"But none of the places I've viewed feels like home." She unlocked the car and looked at Claire over the roof. "And I know, you make a house a home yada yada, but there's certain things you can't take with you."

"Like that gorgeous kitchen island?"

"Like the fact I raised my babies there," she said, climbing behind the wheel.

"Why not stay?" Claire suggested, settling in the passenger seat and strapping into her seatbelt. "Paul said you can keep the house for the girls."

"I know." Clutching the wheel, Sally smiled sadly. "That place doesn't feel like home either. Every time I walk in, I just remember how rubbish my marriage was in the last few years."

"So, you don't want to leave because of the memories?"

"Yeah."

"And you don't want to stay because of the memories?"

"I suppose." Sally twisted the key in the ignition but didn't immediately set off. "Sounds silly when you put it like that."

"There is one thing you could do," Claire said. "Pull a Janet and redecorate the house to within an inch of its life. You don't have to move to change how the house feels."

"I'd be out of a job if more people thought like that." She stared ahead as her fingers tapped on the steering wheel. "Not a bad idea, though. I hadn't thought about it like that."

"What are friends for?"

"Don't think I haven't noticed." Sally set off down the road once the estate agent left the property. "We were talking about your problems, not mine. Have *you* tried to kiss Ryan?"

"Not ... exactly."

"Mate, you either have or haven't."

"There was that time in his art studio with the paint fight, but that was sort of ... mutual?"

"Then I'm not counting it." Sally stretched her neck, trying to see the source of the traffic jam behind which they soon ground to a halt. "I know you, Claire. You're the woman who doesn't notice when a guy is flirting with her."

"Guys never flirt with me."

"Exactly." Sally chuckled. "Last time we were in Manchester, that gorgeous guy with the tan was trying it on with you."

They inched forward as cars pulled out of the jam and zoomed back the way they'd all come.

"What guy?"

"Exactly. You didn't notice." She sighed. "Look, I see this differently."

"Whatever it is, say it."

Sally inhaled, edging forward as more cars exited the jam.

"When it comes to romantic relationships, you really don't have a clue." Sally smiled apologetically. "And I'm not saying I do either, but having a boyfriend was never that important to you. You're laid back, and that's great, but sometimes you just need to grab these things by the…"

Sally clenched the air with one hand and squeezed.

"So, I just … kiss him?" Claire asked. "Unless you're suggesting something else. We're definitely not there yet."

"Kiss him," Sally said firmly. "Trust me, mate; Ryan is crazy about you. Is there any chance you've psyched yourselves out with all this waiting, and neither of you is doing it because the other hasn't done it first?"

Claire sank into her chair, hating how spot-on Sally's assessment was. She didn't hate Sally for saying it. She was glad of the honesty; she hated that she hadn't seen it herself.

"I hadn't thought about it like that."

"Like you said, what are friends for?" Sally slapped Claire's knee. "If we can't hold a mirror up to each other, who can?"

"There's still a chance he's about to end things."

"And there's a greater chance he isn't," Sally said with a disbelieving laugh. "Take it from me, from the way you described it, that argument was mild. It wasn't even an argument. You disagreed with a decision he made. What are you supposed to do? Agree just to placate him?"

"I don't think Ryan would ever expect me to do that."

"Good. Your first tiff always feels more serious than it really is." She rolled down the window and leaned her head out. "Bloody temporary traffic lights are stuck on red. Always roadworks. Forget this. I know another way home."

Sally turned out of the jam and retreated past the house they'd viewed. After some quick turns and roundabouts, they came out on a straight road surrounded by fields.

"For what it's worth," continued Sally, "I think you're right about showing Amelia the card. How can we expect our kids to be honest with us if we're not honest with them?"

"I think Ryan is worried that history is repeating itself." She looked around for her phone. "I found a picture of my fourteenth birthday party last night."

"Is that the one where your mother cut off your fringe and you had to wear that ridiculous hat?"

"I looked fetching."

"You looked like you were about to go off to Ladies Day at the races." Sally laughed. "Still can't find your phone?"

Claire shook her head as she groped around in the footwell.

"I have a feeling I left it at the shop."

"Then I bet Ryan has sent a dozen text messages. If you'd texted him last night, you probably would have squashed this before it had time to fester."

"Maybe," she said, checking the backseat despite not having been there. "I ended up gutting my flat like the Queen was about to come round. That's when I found the pictures."

"Now who's pulling a Janet?" Sally slowed down as a car sped towards them from the opposite direction. "Had any thoughts about your birthday yet?"

"I'm happy to let it pass me—"

The car sped past them without slowing, followed by two more, all identical.

Shiny black paint.

Dark tinted windows.

No licence plates.

Through the rear-view mirror, Claire watched them slow and turn down a lane.

"Eryk's wife thinks she's being followed by black cars," Claire said, slapping the dashboard. "Turn around and follow them."

"Have you lost the plot?"

"Probably." Claire slapped the dash again. "Seeing them once could be nothing. Twice is a coincidence, but that's the third time I've seen them."

"We're nowhere near Northash."

"But considering where we're heading, it looks like that's where they've come from." Her foot tapped as the black cars grew smaller in the mirror. "If we hang back, they'll never know we're following them."

"The question is why."

"To find out where they're coming from," Claire said. "Mysterious black cars suddenly showing up in the village ... aren't you even a little curious?"

Sally's fingers drummed on the wheel as she continued down the road. She ground to a halt and performed a messy three-point turn before speeding back.

"Isn't Anna being behind everything the current consensus?" Sally asked as they trundled down the sloping, bumpy road into the countryside. "I saw the boards on the post office this morning. Looks like she did a number on the place."

"The police mustn't think so," she said, unable to see the black cars ahead as they ventured deeper. "Charged with criminal damage and released on bail."

The road ended at a footbridge over a river in the shallow of a valley. Sally ground to a halt and pulled up a handbrake next to a row of allotments.

"Dead end." Sally clutched the steering wheel as she looked around. "Did I miss another turning?"

Shielding her eyes from the setting sun, Claire climbed out. The black cars had vanished.

"You've had your excursion," Sally said through her rolled down window. "Let's just get back."

"One second."

Claire walked down to the footbridge, too narrow for a car to pass over. Clutching the metal railing, she peered at the gushing river far below, wondering if they had missed a road. Wherever the cars had driven, they'd be long gone now.

"You're right," Claire said as she walked back up to the car. "I was being silly, anyway."

"Perhaps not." Sally climbed out of the car and pointed down a lane bending around the back of the

AGATHA FROST

allotments. "I heard car doors slam down there. You wear glasses. Can you see anything?"

"They don't give me super vision." She pushed them up and squinted down the lane. "No, I can't see—"

Where the lane curved, a bright, artificial light banished the dusky darkness. Claire and Sally looked at each other with arched brows. Without a word, they set off.

"You're right," Sally whispered. "I am curious."

As tight as the lane was, two trenches the width of tyres ran the whole way down, turned to mud by the recent rain. They hopped between the dry sections, sticking to the bushes, fences, and chicken wire surrounding the various allotments.

"What the…" Sally's voice trailed off as they peered around the bend. "Have they robbed a brewery?"

The three black cars were parked in front of a block of five storage units. Light poured from the only unit with its shutter open, giving them a clear view of the hundreds, if not thousands, of alcohol bottles lined up on metal shelves inside. One guy pulled bottles from a shelf while ticking things off on a clipboard; the others boxed them. The men were moving around, but Claire counted at least ten.

"They haven't robbed a brewery," she whispered. "They *are* the brewery."

"The fake alcohol!"

"We should go," said Claire, gulping. "The alcohol might be fake, but I don't think those guns are."

While the men worked inside, two more patrolled back and forth with shotguns, their eyes constantly scanning.

Claire clutched Sally's arm. "Is it me or—"

"It's not you," Sally replied. "He's looking right at us."

Without another word, they returned the way they'd come. They tried dancing over the muddy patches as best they could, until Sally glanced over her shoulder. She clutched Claire's hand and dragged her along at a sprint. The opening of the muddy lane came into view, as did Sally's car, suddenly lit up by more glowing light.

"Damn!" Sally muttered, tugging Claire through an allotment gate seconds before another black car turned down the lane. "Yeah, I'm not curious anymore. We need to get out of here."

As the daylight quickly faded, they crept through the quiet allotment in the direction of Sally's car. The black cars arrived in an endless stream, but they didn't all go down the lane.

"They've blocked me in!" Sally whispered. "Bloody hell, Claire. What have you dragged me—"

Claire wrapped her hand around Sally's mouth and pulled her down behind a bed of thriving cabbages. The allotment door creaked open, and the gunman walked in. Pinning herself against the wooden planting box, Claire clutched Sally's hand and held her breath.

"I think he's gone," Sally whispered as another creaky hinge whinged further down. "How are we going to get my car out?"

"Maybe they'll move?" She peered around the planter. "Either way, I don't think we should stay here. Get up a map on your phone."

Sally groaned, clenching one eye.

"It's in the car, isn't it?"

"I didn't bring my bag," she said. "I didn't expect we'd be chased down by a gunman."

"Oh, I did."

"*What?*"

"I just wanted to see the look on your face."

"Are you—"

"Joking." She looked around the allotment, glad to see a gate on the other side. "The further we can get from the guns, the better."

Crouched low to the ground, they slipped through the opposite gate. It brought them onto a tight path almost swallowed by bushes, and beyond that, the rushing river echoed through the valley.

"What do we—"

Birds fled the trees as a loud bang cut through the air. This time, Claire didn't wonder if it was fireworks.

"That was a *warning* shot!" a man cried. "The next one won't be."

Sally yanked Claire through a gap in the bushes and onto the other side. There wasn't another path to speak of, only a few inches of flat ground before the mud gave way to the steep slope down to the river.

"You shouldn't have come here," the man cried again, closer. "*Go!*"

"I just want to know where my dad is," a familiar, shaky voice replied.

Sally and Claire looked at each other, wide-eyed and holding their breath.

"We don't explain ourselves to you," the man said over the click of a shotgun emptying its casings. "Are you trying to test my aim?"

Further down the river, the silhouette of a skinny man scrambled onto the footbridge, tripping over himself as he ran away.

Still crouching, Claire turned to confirm the identity of the person from whom the familiar voice had come.

The mud licked the heel of her shoe.

And then she fell.

CHAPTER FOURTEEN

*I*t might have been summer, but the river was freezing all the same. Claire's ankle, on the other hand, burned hot.

Water rushed into her ears, fizzing like static. She couldn't blink fast enough to keep it out of her eyes, and she slapped a hand to her face seconds too late to save her glasses from the force that ripped them off.

Hands gripped around her arms, pulling her up before she could think about saving herself. She gasped and sputtered, colder than she'd been since winter.

"Bloody hell, Claire," Sally muttered as she dragged Claire out of the water. "Are you alright? You'd already gone before I could reach out to help you."

Sally hauled her onto the muddy bank, where the

canopy of trees blocked any remaining daylight and left them in darkness.

A jacket went around her shoulders, and she realised the second pair of hands belonged to Leo. He put his finger to his lips and pointed to the bushes at the top of the slope.

Too much water in her ears to hear the whispers.

Too blind without her glasses to see more than shadows.

"We're lucky they didn't hear that," Leo said, propping Claire up when she winced at placing weight on her right foot. "Is it broken?"

"Sprained, I think," she said, wiggling it as much as she could. "I fell on my backside."

"I've never seen anything like it." Sally propped her up on the other side. "You rolled. Backwards. All the way down."

Sally stared at her, biting her lip as though holding back tears, though the shaking corners hinted at something else.

"That really happened, didn't it?" Claire stared up at the incline. "I just went backside over head the whole way down that hill."

Claire stifled a laugh.

Sally's finally sprang free.

"This isn't funny," Leo whispered, his soft voice lacking any authority. "We need to get out of here."

Claire and Sally coughed away their laughter as they clambered up the other side of the bank. It was just as steep but had more twigs and rocks than mud to provide purchase. At the top, they reached a flat path. An even steeper gravelled slope coiled high into the trees, but without her glasses, she couldn't tell where it led.

She loved those glasses.

"What are you doing here?" Leo demanded.

"What are *you* doing here?" Claire fired back, hopping on her left foot to a wooden fence she could lean against. "And of course this side has a fence to stop people rolling backwards into the bloody river."

"I asked first."

"Leo," Claire said sternly. "I've been trying to find you for days. And now, here you are at the source of Northash's newest favourite tipple-supplier, demanding to see your father. And let's not forget the guns!" She took a calming breath. "You've been lying to me this whole time. I know it. What's going on?"

Sally gave Claire a thumbs up behind Leo's back before folding her arms, attempting to look somewhat tough.

"I'm in a bit of a mess," Leo said, his bottom lip

wobbling, "and I don't know how to get out of it. I'm scared, Claire."

Sally's arms dropped, all pretence at toughness vanishing.

"That might be the most honest thing you've said to me all week," Claire said. "Let's walk and talk. Well, you walk. I'll hop."

Fortunately for Claire and Sally, Leo knew exactly where they were. Apparently, he was part of a flourishing orienteering club Claire hadn't even known existed.

Unfortunately for Claire, the only way to get home without backtracking through the valley was to keep going up. Even with Sally and Leo's support on either side of her, she could only hop so fast.

"A few months ago, Eryk said we were switching suppliers," Leo started as they traversed the gravel. "I didn't think anything of it, in the beginning. Everything seemed to be the same. A few people returned things. I thought that was normal. I'd only been there for a few months. But then ... men started showing up."

"Those men?" Claire asked, squinting towards the blurry lights of the storage units.

"Those men," he said, nodding. "They said we were in debt. The post office. At first, I thought they were bailiffs. Eryk always turned up and got rid of them before they made a scene."

"Eryk owed them money?" Sally asked. "That doesn't sound right."

"He owed them *thousands*," Leo confirmed. "He took out loans with them that he couldn't pay back. Selling their products was his way of trying to get on their good side while he repaid them. But he couldn't keep up with the repayments, and they kept upping the interest. Every day since Eryk died, they've been hounding us, following us. My dad was trying to sever ties and get them off our backs, but they wouldn't take no for an answer. The raid only made things worse."

"They don't seem like the most ... reasonable of people," said Claire.

"They're not." He gulped. "I haven't seen my dad since the police released him. I thought if I came here, I could reason with them. See if they knew where he was. I think ... I think they took him."

"Why wouldn't your dad tell the police?"

"Because they threatened to kill us."

"Is that what happened to Eryk?"

Leo nodded.

They reached the top of the gravel path, only to find another steep slope, though at least this one flattened out towards fuzzy yellow streetlights glowing against the outlines of buildings.

"You should report your dad as missing," Claire said, breaking a long silence as the climbing evened out. "They can't help find him if they don't know."

"He specifically told me not to do that if anything like this happened. You've seen what they're capable of."

Claire had no idea where they were, but they hadn't driven that far out of Northash on the other side of the valley. To think there were such underbellies hidden deep away behind allotments in the countryside terrified her. Knowing they'd hawked their wares to her fellow villagers, her father being one of them, knocked her sick.

"Where does Tomek fit into this?" Claire asked as they walked down the lit-up road of semi-detached houses with fenced in front gardens and TVs on behind every window. "He made you lie for him, didn't he?"

Leo nodded. "He took the money from the till and told me not to tell anyone. He said the police wouldn't be suspicious. They'd expect it."

"So, it *was* a fake burglary." Claire let out a breath, vindicated. "I knew it."

"I'm lucky I don't buy my red wine from the post

office," said Sally. "Not that they sell mine."

"Snob." Arm around Sally's shoulders, Claire flicked her ear. "Leo, how did Tomek's prints get on the gun?"

"I-I told you," he muttered. "There was a struggle."

Once again, he was frogmarching her, and although he was helping rather than ejecting her from the shop, the same feeling twisted in her belly.

Lies.

He'd been too honest tonight.

Now she could easily tell the difference.

"How are things with Berna?" she asked, intentionally not beating around the bush. "She told me you were together."

A lie for a lie.

"She did?" He scratched at his neck with his free hand as they left the housing estate. "Things aren't great right now. Terrible, if I'm being honest.

A lie for a truth.

"How did you meet?"

"The post office," he said with a genuine smile. "She came in to see her father. I'd only worked there for a month. The moment I saw her, I thought she was the most beautiful girl I'd ever seen."

"Leo," Sally said in a sickly tone. "That's so sweet."

"Her dad never showed up," he continued. "It was near closing and she asked if I wanted to go for a drink at the pub. I thought she was joking. I *asked* if she was joking." He paused as Claire and Sally winced. "She wasn't. I don't know what happened we just … clicked."

"Chemistry," Sally said across Claire. "You either have it or you don't, and it's probably better if you can't even explain it. It took meeting a man with whom I had it to realise I married a man with whom I didn't."

"What man?" Claire asked.

"Oh." Sally scrambled. "Just some guy. I'll tell you about it later."

Claire had a strong inkling who 'some guy' was, but she kept her thoughts to herself. She almost congratulated Leo on Berna's pregnancy but bit her tongue at the last moment. She didn't know if he knew. *She* wasn't supposed to know. It wasn't like Berna had told her.

They were still ten miles from Northash, a fact Leo kept to himself until they reached a bus stop he knew would take them home. Thankfully, he had money as well as orienteering skills.

After forty minutes of ankle-resting silence, which only made her notice the throbbing more, they climbed off the bus at the stop outside the factory on the hill, the line's only stop in Northash. Rather than taking the steep Warton Lane path, they risked the shortcut through Ian Baron's farm; thankfully, he seemed to be asleep.

The whole cul-de-sac was dark, curtains free of twitching, except for the one house with lights on in every room.

"Oh my days!" Janet exclaimed, jumping up from the dining table as Claire hopped through the back door. "*Alan*! She's here! Claire's here!"

Janet pulled Claire into a hug, river-damp clothes and all. Over her mother's shoulder, the LED screen on the oven let her know it was four minutes from eleven. Claire hadn't considered the time – or even that anyone would have noticed her absence.

"Been up to trouble?" her father asked, his tone not jovial enough to hide the clear worry in his eyes. "You're wet."

Janet hurried out of the room as Claire collapsed into a chair at the dining table. Sally fetched a bag of frozen sprouts, wrapping them around the ankle Claire obligingly lifted and rested on another chair.

"I found the source of the suspect booze," Claire said, glancing at the two bottles still on the sideboard. "Not intentionally, but I think Leo could point to it on a map." She smiled at him. "I don't think we would have got out of there without him."

"Claire fell down a hill into a river," Sally announced, almost proudly. "You should have seen it."

"Fell is too kind," Claire admitted. "I rolled backwards."

"Backside over head?"

"Backside over head."

Like Sally earlier, her father struggled to look sympathetic while holding back a reactionary laugh.

"I kept these for emergencies after you moved out." Janet dropped a pile of crisply ironed clothes onto the table. "You'll catch your death."

"It's August," Claire said, picking up the khaki t-shirt she'd spent twenty minutes looking for a fortnight ago. "What kind of emergencies?"

"Oh, like this one right now."

"Good point."

After throwing back the painkillers her mother offered, Claire locked herself in the downstairs bathroom and got acquainted with a hand towel. Once in her dry clothes, she felt more like herself.

As nights went, this had to be the strangest she'd experienced in a very long time.

She left the downstairs bathroom just as the front door opened. Ryan burst in, still dressed in his gym clothes. He stopped in his tracks and stared disbelievingly at Claire, apparently oblivious to the front door still gaping open behind him.

"You're here," he said, clasping his hands behind his head. "I've been looking everywhere for you."

"You have?"

"I went to the shop to apologise as soon as I finished work," he said, "but you weren't there. I called you, but I heard your phone ringing in the shop. With everything that's been going on, I didn't know what to think."

Sally walked past and through to the living room. As she closed the door behind her, she clenched the air with her fist.

"So, you've been looking for me, eh?" Claire asked, taking a step towards him. "Searching high and low?"

"All night," he said, dropping his hands. "The whole village. I've been so worried."

She clenched the air by her side and took a deep breath as she looked at Ryan's lips, glistening under the hallway light.

She'd stared at those lips countless times, always wanting to kiss them and never once acting on it.

Tonight, she'd break the habit of a lifetime.

Grabbing the straps of Ryan's vest, she pulled him in, and like two jigsaw pieces fitting together, they kissed.

Fireworks didn't go off.

Time didn't stop.

The cul-de-sac didn't melt away.

But oh, she was relieved.

Relieved to be over the hurdle.

Relieved that kissing him felt so *right*.

Behind them, a throat cleared on the stairs. Claire lingered at Ryan's lips for another second before reluctantly withdrawing. Releasing Ryan's vest, she turned to her pinched-lipped grandmother standing three steps up. Mean Moreen loomed over them, her white hair cascading over a tightly fastened silk dressing gown – black, of course.

Claire hadn't heard her walk down. Perhaps there was something to Granny Greta's insinuations that Moreen could transform into a bat at the drop of a hat.

"You are not dead, then, I see," she said coldly.

"Not this time."

"You are blocking the stairs."

As Claire stepped aside, Ryan's arm slipped around her waist, though his eyes remained on the carpet as Moreen stalked past them.

"Gran?" Claire called as Moreen made her way to the kitchen.

"Grand*mother*."

"Grandmother." Claire resisted rolling her eyes. "Is

it true that you used to work at the factory?"

Moreen stiffened, her hands clasped at her waist as she peered indirectly back at them.

"Yes," she said rigidly. "Briefly."

Claire smiled as she watched a layer of Moreen's self-imposed superiority melt away.

"Fascinating." Claire wrapped her hand around Ryan's. "I never knew we had so much in common."

For most grandmothers, such a statement would invoke a smile, maybe even a hug. Moreen only glared at her from the corner of her eye, nostrils flared and ready to breathe fire. She croaked an acknowledgement and continued to the kitchen.

"You almost got her there." Ryan pulled her down onto the steps as they laughed like schoolchildren. "Claire?"

"Yeah?"

Ryan's fingers slid up her cheek, and he pulled her in for another kiss. This time, her mind slipped backwards. They were on the same step from the sixteenth birthday party picture.

The hallway looked different.

They looked different.

Things were different.

This was different.

Another tart throat clearing pulled them apart and

AGATHA FROST

Moreen squeezed between them with a glass of water. She floated upstairs, leaving them to laugh under their breaths, hiding their faces in each other's necks.

Maybe not so different.

"I made cocoa!" Janet announced from the kitchen. "Get it while it's hot."

To Claire's surprise, two pairs of eyes appeared through the bannister at the top of the stairs. Amelia and Hugo, dressed in their pyjamas, crept into view, their eyes bleary with sleep.

"Hi, Claire," Hugo said. "You're okay."

"I am," she replied. "I hope I didn't worry you."

"I told you she'd be fine," Amelia said with a yawn. "Where are your glasses?"

"Lost them in a river."

"Cool."

"You might as well come down and have some cocoa." Janet squeezed through Claire and Ryan, carrying a steaming mug. "There's squirty cream and marshmallows."

Janet stuck to the wall to make room for Amelia and Hugo to run down. Ryan followed them into the kitchen.

"I looked after them while Ryan looked for you," Janet said, pausing on the steps. "He didn't stop. He cares about you a lot."

"Yeah, he does." Claire smiled. "You can't possibly be taking that to your mother."

Janet snorted. "Can you imagine? No. Ash is on the sofa bed in the computer room," she said, carrying on to the next step. "After our last conversation, I realised I couldn't leave him alone in that house. I don't know what the next move will be, but for now, that child needs a few days to just *be*."

In the kitchen, Ryan squirted cream directly into Amelia's mouth before leaving a dollop on her nose. She laughed, pushed him away, and threw a pink marshmallow at him.

Ryan's being a father was, of course, the biggest difference between the present and the past, and Claire loved seeing what it brought out in him.

"What's this?" Claire asked, joining her father at the dining table. "Planning a walk?"

"I asked young Leo to circle where he thought the storage buildings are." He jabbed his finger at a red circle in the middle of a large map.

"Where is he?"

"Isn't he here? He was a moment ago, until…" Alan glanced around the kitchen. "Until I told him an officer was on their way to take statements about what you witnessed. Is it true they had guns?"

"Shotguns."

"Like the post office."

Claire nodded, staring at the red circle.

"I know that face," Alan said with a grin. "I invented that face. What's on your mind, little one?"

"It might be nothing."

"It might be something."

"A feeling," she said. "That everything isn't as it seems. It would make sense for this gang to be behind Eryk's shooting. A neat bow."

"But?"

"Tomek." She took the chair next to him. "Who killed Tomek, and why? And why were his prints on the gun? I asked Leo, but I'm certain he was lying. He told me he was scared, and I believed him."

"Of what?" he asked, leaning in. "Or should I say, of whom?"

"I wish I…"

Claire's voice drifted off as she noticed the positioning of the red circle on the map. Clutching the table, she stood and leaned in. Without her glasses, the details never came into focus. She snagged her father's frames and held them up to her eyes. The prescription wasn't identical, but it wasn't far off.

Sally, a chunky knit blanket from the sitting room wrapped around her shoulders, joined them in staring at the circle.

"That's not right," Claire said, tapping the marked spot. "There's no river on here. Or allotments."

"And there weren't that many houses," said Sally, dragging her fingertip over the map. "We viewed a house over here. Maybe he got it wrong?"

"Twenty miles wrong?" said Alan.

"He's trying to throw us off the scent." Claire dropped heavily into the chair and returned her father's glasses. "He knew exactly where we were the entire time; he guided us home. He's lying."

"Something else he said set off my alarm bells," Sally said, circling the allotments on the map and drawing several arrows to it. "That comment about Eryk being in debt."

"You said it didn't sound right."

"Because it doesn't," she said, popping the lid on the pen. "Eryk was viewing houses with my company last month, and the price range in which he was shopping always needs financial preapproval. We're talking the last step before houses become full-on mansions. You can't fake those numbers, and loan shark money certainly wouldn't pass."

"Could have got into debt quickly?" Claire mused. "Or Leo is lying about that too? Either way, I don't think we can't trust a single thing he said."

CHAPTER FIFTEEN

*T*he adrenaline and painkillers had worn off by sunrise, and Claire winced the second she threw back her bedcovers and her foot touched the floor.

"Nope," she said, immediately crawling back into the soft warmth of her bed. "Not today."

Damon was far too capable of running the show for her to spend a day grinning through the pain. After she texted him, he came up with breakfast, and they ate bacon and egg sandwiches sprawled on her bed while a classic episode of *The Simpsons* played on Channel 4. He fed the cats; put painkillers, coffee, and a glass of water next to her bed; and went down to man the shop.

Alone in her flat and wearing her thick, black-rimmed spare glasses, she snuggled up with Domino and Sid in bed while *The Simpsons* played back-to-back, pausing only for adverts. She hadn't spent a Saturday this way since her days at the factory. Compared to how she'd been spending her days lately, the normalcy was refreshing.

Before leaving her parents' house the night before, she'd given the police her statement about the gun-wielding booze boys. On reflection, following the cars had proven to be one of her more reckless impulsive decisions, though she hoped the experience might bring about some justice.

Today, she was content to be lazy. She'd have been fine to spend the day alone with only the company of the cats, Homer, and the indistinct chatter in the shop below. As it happened, she didn't need to.

"I bought all your favourites," Ryan said, dropping onto the bed as he tipped out the contents of a plastic bag. "Wotsits, Starburst, Cadburys, and Vimto."

Ryan's knowledge of her favourite things was frozen in their youth. Not that she didn't still love them, but it was almost touching that, in some way, Ryan still thought of her like that.

"Flying visit?" she asked as he curled up on the bed and popped open a packet of cheesy Wotsits.

"Pulled a sickie," he admitted through the first

mouthful. "With the hours I put in at the gym, I've earned it. Your mum's put the kids to work helping clean the windows"

"Child labour." Claire picked up a packet of cheese puffs. "Classic Janet."

"They seemed to be enjoying it." The Vimto hissed as he twisted the cap. "Means I'm yours for the day. If you want me?"

"Nah," she said, grinning. "Bugger off."

A fluffy scatter cushion bounced off her head, and she launched it straight back.

"You're abusing your patient."

"It's your ankle that hurts," he said, sucking the caked-on cheese dust from his finger. "I could give you a foot rub?"

"You know how I feel about people touching my feet." She shuddered. "Pass."

"Oh, yeah," he said, grazing his finger along the sole of her left foot. "I forgot how ticklish you are."

"Ryan!" Claire jerked her leg away. "I have no problem ruining your pretty face with the heel of my foot."

"Oh, it's pretty now, is it?" His grin widened as he unwrapped a red Starburst. "You're funny."

"Funny looking?"

"You know I think you're beautiful."

Claire's heart skipped a beat as the jovial, teasing nature of their conversation took a sudden turn. Not only did she not *know* it, she hadn't even considered the possibility that he'd think that way about her.

"I didn't know that," she said, swallowing around the sudden dryness. "You've never said it before."

"Haven't I?" His eyes widened in what appeared to be genuine surprise. "I've always thought it."

Claire was about to ask if always meant always since his return or *always* always. The sound of someone jogging up the staircase delayed the question.

"Oh," Sally said, taking a step inside and immediately freezing. "Not interrupting, am I?"

"Only Starburst and *The Simpsons*."

"Got any green ones left?" she asked, joining them on the bed.

"Who likes the green ones?" Ryan passed her the bag. "Red is where it's at."

"You're both wrong because it's actually purple," she said, noticing Sally's quietness as she stared into the bag without digging around. "Mate?"

"I'm being followed," she whispered, putting the bag down without taking any. "I just finished my second viewing of the morning, and I've already seen three of those black cars. They know who we are."

"How?" Claire sat up. "They never got a proper look at us."

"My car, maybe?" Sally scratched at her hair. "It was fine when my Mum took me to get it at the crack of dawn this morning. Place was all quiet. Can you find out who owns a car from a licence plate? I thought they'd have been arrested by now. We told the police everything they needed to know."

"It's never that simple."

Glad the painkillers had taken the edge off, Claire used various pieces of furniture to make her way to the front window. Stroking Domino as she sunbathed in the windowsill, Claire stared at the Saturday bustle below.

Four black cars encased the clock tower in a square.

"Your dad said it might be an intimidation technique," Sally whispered, appearing next to her. "Are they going to kill us? Are we next?"

"We're going to be fine," she replied, stepping away from the window. "When did you see my dad?"

"He's downstairs helping Damon."

Claire ventured down for the first time all morning. The usual Saturday busyness had returned, a stark contrast to the long, quiet hours following Eryk's shooting only a week earlier.

"I see them, little one," said Alan when she joined him behind the counter. "Don't you worry. Harry's getting everything into place so they can strike. They've had eyes on the storage units since sunrise. Once they get the go ahead from above, this will all be over."

"So, they *do* think the murders were gang-related?" she whispered, smiling at one of her semi-regulars as Damon served her. "Have they got anything we don't know?"

"Other than the connection of the fake alcohol and the gun, no," he said with a sigh, "but maybe that's all they need. If there's a case to be built, they'll be able to start assembling it today."

A trio of women crowding the star candle display moved, revealing a woman with a red flower in her hair. Anna sniffed a rose petal candle, one of the leftovers from the month before. Claire had moved them to a smaller display.

"Do you like it?" asked Claire as she approached.

"Yes." Anna's eyes narrowed. "I have the same one at home. Do I know you?"

"This is my shop," she explained. "We haven't spoken before, but I know—"

"Ah, yes, I know who you are now." Anna put the lid back on the jar and returned it. "You're the meddler, asking everyone in my family questions about Eryk. You must have been my husband's mistress."

Claire leaned against the stand for support and lifted a placating hand.

"I don't think we're on the same page here," she said quickly. "I wasn't having an affair with your husband. My mother, Janet, worked for him."

"Oh." Anna looked her up and down again. "You're just his type. I assumed it must be you. Why are you asking so many questions? Leo told me you are harassing him."

"I wouldn't go that far," she said under her breath. "I just want to know what's going on in the village, like everyone else. Like I'm sure you do. It's been a rough week, but I don't need to tell you that. I'm terribly sorry for what you've gone through."

"Thank you." Anna raised a smile. "And yes, it has been the most difficult week, and I haven't made it easier for myself."

Anna looked through the wall as though seeing the destruction she'd caused at the post office. She probably didn't even remember taking a swing at Claire with the golf club.

"My family are close," she said, once again picking up the jar and pulling off the lid. "Even as our numbers dwindle, we are loyal to each other. We don't hurt each other. Whatever you think happened, you don't know the half of it."

Sniffing the candle, Anna half-turned and looked through the window out the corner of her eye. Claire couldn't be sure, but she seemed to be checking if the black cars were still there.

"You mean the fake alcohol?" Claire pushed. "And the gang?"

"How do you know about that?"

"Gossip gets around quickly," she lied. "It seems Eryk got himself into a bit of a mess."

Anna's eyes snapped back to Claire as the candle jar slipped from her fingers. The glass shattered on contact. When the naked pink candle stopped rolling away, silence had fallen over the shop.

"My husband did no such thing," Anna said in a harsh whisper. "How *dare* you!"

"I'm sorry, I—"

"Everything alright here?" Alan interjected as Damon hurried over with a dustpan and brush.

"Just an accident, Dad."

Anna didn't avert her furious stare; every flicker of rage was clear in her icy blue eyes. Claire didn't need to ask to know how much she'd offended the widow. Hearing her words, she was reminded of Em's comment about choosing the right time to show someone the picture you'd painted of the situation.

"Stay away from my family," said Anna, pointing an accusatory finger. "That's a warning."

"Now, now." Alan held up his hands between them. "There's no need for threats, is there?"

Anna's finger didn't drop.

Her gaze didn't waver.

Without a shadow of a doubt, Claire believed the threat. She'd seen Anna swinging that golf club, after all.

"*Idiota.*"

Anna left, and Claire didn't need a translator to know what she'd just been called. Had her idiocy been that offensive? She watched Anna turn right towards the post office. The closest black car sailed after her.

"You struck a nerve," Damon said, sweeping up the last of the glass as the customers awakened around them. "What did you say to her?"

"That Eryk got himself into trouble with the gang." She rearranged the candles to disguise that one was missing. "It's like she was more upsct by the insinuation than the fact I'd said it. Almost like this was the first she'd heard of it?"

"Maybe Eryk didn't keep her abreast of his illegal activity?" Damon used the display to pull himself up.

"Don't let it get to you. The police are on it now. Like your dad said, it will all be over today."

"That's not exactly what he said." She took the dustpan from him. "I think he's struggling on the till. I'll take this out."

Whether it was the painkillers kicking in or the sudden flood of adrenaline, her ankle didn't seem to hurt as much. She took the dustpan straight out to the back yard and swept it into the bin.

The pink label stood out against the bin bags.

"I have the same one at home," Anna had said.

Claire hadn't been sure if Anna meant one of her candles, specifically, or just a rose-scented candle in general. She hadn't sold many since she'd moved it from centre stage to make way for the summer scents, and obviously Anna hadn't entered the shop to purchase the candle herself.

One of the last rose petal candles she'd sold had been to Duncan, when he'd come in looking for a last-minute gift. Could it be a coincidence? Or had Duncan been the man talking to Anna during the phone call Claire had overheard in the gym showers?

Were they secretly together?

Did Anna kill Eryk to end her marriage?

If not for Tomek's death, too, she might have believed it. Murdering her husband was one thing, but murdering her son and making it look like a suicide?

Given how strongly Anna had defended her family just now, every fibre of Claire's being rejected the idea.

Soft cries derailed Claire's thoughts, drawing her to the back alley. Leo sobbed into his hands behind the post office, perched on an upturned crate from Wilson's Greengrocers. Seeing him took her aback; the post office wasn't open.

"She's left me," he choked out after Claire cleared her throat to announce her presence. "Berna's left me. She's going to Poland with her mum."

Claire rushed to his side. She'd envisioned pinning Leo up against a wall and demanding the truth next time she saw him, but how could she do that now?

Lies or not, heartbreak like this couldn't be faked. Seventeen years ago, she'd been in an all too similar state after sending Ryan off to the airport and the Spanish beauty who'd stolen his heart.

"She's pregnant with my baby," he said, melting into Claire's side. "How can I stop her?"

"I don't think you can." She ran a hand over his hair. "I'm sorry, Leo. Did she explain why?"

"After everything t-that's happened, she wants to be with her f-family." He gasped for breath around the shuddering aftermath of his sobs, dragging tears from his cheeks with the back of his hand. "I said I'd go with her, but she told me it wouldn't work. I love her, Claire. I love her so much."

As Leo cried his heart out, Claire could only hold him and rub soothing circles against his trembling back. She considered offering the usual platitudes – he was still young; he'd find someone else; there were plenty of fish in the sea –but her conversation with Anna was still fresh, and this wasn't the time.

And it wasn't necessarily true, either.

She wasn't about to add to the many dishonesties lately by lying to a young man with a freshly broken heart.

"They've ruined my life," he said with a darker edge to his voice. "That family's ruined my life. Her mum is taking her away from me now, just like her dad tried to split us up before he was shot." He pointed to faded remnants of his black eye. "We thought the baby would show him how serious we were. We were going to wait, but Tomek overheard Berna telling her mother, and he went straight to Eryk. It only made things worse. I'm glad he's dead. I'm glad they're both dead."

Claire pulled away from Leo slightly.

"No," he protested, shaking his head. "I just heard that back. I didn't kill them. No, Claire. I didn't do it. I wouldn't. I couldn't. I—"

"But you know who did," she said, putting more space between them. "You're protecting someone, aren't you? You lied for Tomek about the money, and you know who shot Eryk. You were the only one there, Leo."

"I ... I ..."

"It was Berna," she said, her mouth drying. "You're protecting Berna. She killed her father for—"

"*What?*" Leo leapt to his feet. "Berna has *nothing* to do with this!"

"Then who are you protecting?" Claire cried. "Leo, this isn't a game. Tell me! We can fix this."

Leo stared at her, his mouth working as he tried to form a word. Claire mimicked the movement with her lips.

"M?" she pressed, grabbing his shoulders. "Is it someone in the gang? Someone you know?"

A forced cough echoed from above them. They turned to the source, the open window above the post office. The curtains fluttered in the breeze, showing just enough of a bruised and battered face for Claire to recognise Duncan.

Leo tore away and slammed the gate. The last time she'd been in the post office, he'd mentioned his father being upstairs. Assuming Leo meant a storeroom or something, she hadn't thought much of it.

But it wasn't.

She knew it wasn't.

Her mother had talked about the empty flat above the post office for years.

If he wasn't protecting Berna, who else could it be?

"M?" she mouthed to herself, gazing up at the window as Duncan slammed it shut.

CHAPTER SIXTEEN

*T*his time, Claire knew how reckless she was being. Even with her sore ankle, this knowledge didn't stop her from following Leo through the gate.

And into the post office.

And up the staircase.

She'd been going about everything wrong – focusing on the wrong people, focusing on the wrong family. Leo was the key, but she'd been wrong about which lock he fit into.

"Claire?" Leo cried, pushing her back through the door when she walked into the flat. "You can't be here."

The flat was identical in size and layout to the one above the candle shop, though it more closely resembled hers before she'd redecorated. The walls were dark and floral, the floorboards exposed and bare of carpet. Where she'd placed her sofa and TV, this flat had only a blow-up bed and half a dozen bags of clothes.

"You can't be here," Leo repeated. "Please, Claire. Go."

"You were going to say something beginning with M."

Peering around Leo towards the ajar bathroom door, Claire saw Duncan wince as he dabbed a soaked cotton ball against one of the many fresh cuts on his face.

Through the mirror, Duncan's gaze locked on Claire, and he spun around. She saw the cogs working in the moments before a smile lifted his bruised cheeks. Had that tooth always been missing? The fresh blood suggested not.

"Hi, neighbour," he said, his breath rattling. "Come to borrow some sugar?"

Neighbour.

He'd called her that when she'd first spoken to him in the post office below.

"It was you, wasn't it?" she asked, before turning to Leo. "You were going to say, 'my dad', weren't you?"

"What was me?" Duncan asked, drying his bloody hands on a white towel as he stepped out of the bathroom. "Please, share what's on your mind."

"Claire..." Leo shook his head. "Please go."

She couldn't drop the scent now. Not with the source of the stench standing right in front of her.

She pulled away from Leo and followed Duncan into the sitting room area. He perched on the edge of the blow-up mattress and wrapped a bandage around his hand.

"Looks like you gave as good as you got," she said, nodding at the blood seeping through at the knuckles. "Shouldn't you be at the hospital?"

"I'll worry about me." He gulped down an entire bottle of water until the plastic crunched to nothing. "So, enlighten me, Claire. What exactly did I do?"

"You flew under the radar," she said, looking through the curtain-less window at the busy square below. "I saw a light on up here when I was outside the pub. It didn't register at the time; I'd forgotten this flat was meant to be empty. But it's not, is it? Because you're living here. The reason I didn't see a gunman fleeing down the back alley was because that gunman didn't flee, he just came upstairs. You would have known how to turn the cameras off. You would have known when Eryk would be here. You weren't in Yorkshire, you were here. You shot Eryk, then hid up here."

Duncan smirked, his tongue poking at a cut in his lip.

"What a fantastic story. Tell me, Claire," he said, "why did I shoot Eryk?"

"You were having an affair with his wife."

"I'd hardly call it an affair." He laughed. "A fling, if that. Anna took it too seriously. I just wanted to get to Eryk."

"Because he was filling the post office with fake alcohol?" She looked around the musty flat. "No, that doesn't seem right, does it? Eryk was off viewing mansions, while you're … here. On a blow-up bed. You brought the fake alcohol to Northash to satisfy those men. Not Eryk. You."

"You speak as though Eryk wasn't fine with it," he scoffed. "Like any good businessman, Eryk could appreciate a cost-cutting opportunity. He didn't understand the seriousness of the people supplying the product, but he soon found out."

"And you're part of the gang?"

"Part of it?" Duncan's chest heaved as he laughed. "Don't be stupid. Would they do this to me if I were one of them? I was just another idiot they could milk for interest payments. Without my stake in this post office, I would have been dead long ago. I couldn't pay back what I borrowed, but my thirty percent share here meant I could still make money for them."

"If Eryk was fine with it, why shoot him?"

"I never said I did."

"But you did."

"I did." He nodded. "I didn't intend to kill him. I merely wanted to scare him after he had an attack of conscience. He wanted to go legit. He said it was only a matter of time before someone got sick and things blew up in our faces. It turns out he was right, he just wasn't around to see it."

"Because you killed him."

"Collateral damage." Duncan coughed, and dabbing his fingers on his lips pulled away blood. "They gave me a shotgun. Told me to scare him. He needed to go along with it. We were in too deep to suddenly stop. They'd never allow it. They've lost too many sellers lately. Too many raids. A little village post office was supposed to be the *last* place the police would look. I needed to show their strength. It was supposed to be a warning shot."

"Through the chest?"

"Eryk told me he wasn't opening the post office on Saturday morning. He wanted to clear the shelves of bottles," he said. "I thought it would be the perfect time to deliver the message loud and clear. People would think it was a burglary, but Eryk would know the truth. I waited in the yard before bursting in to play the part when I heard the bottles clinking."

"I saw you," she said, half-laughing. "You blocked the gate with a bin."

"Ah, that was *you* trying to get in?" Duncan's eyes narrowed as a smirk grew to reveal another tooth barely hanging on. "Almost busted me before I had chance for the big show. Unfortunately, Tomek had similar ideas. I didn't know Eryk had him here, training to take over from your mother."

"So, there *was* a struggle," Claire said, looking at Leo as he paced in the kitchen. "You weren't lying about that. You just didn't want to tell me who Tomek was struggling with. He didn't want you to shoot his father."

"And yet the fool caused just that," Duncan said, coughing again. "I thought it would be Eryk and Leo, and maybe your mother. Not a threat amongst them. But Tomek? Overconfident, just like his father."

Somewhere outside the flat, Claire heard her father shouting her name. She had no idea how Duncan would react if she made a run for it. Besides, the truth was too close to leave now.

"The gun went off," Duncan continued. "My finger was on the trigger, but it wasn't hard to convince Tomek it was his fault. When he suggested taking the money, I knew I had him. I promised to cut him in on the business, and that sealed the deal. In the time it took Eryk to stumble to the door, the three of us agreed to stick to the story."

"You convinced Tomek he murdered his own father?" Claire's stomach twisted, threatening to expel bacon and egg sandwich, cheesy Wotsits, and purple Starburst. "That's sick."

"It's business." He clutched his ribs. "Tomek was a loose cannon. I should have known it wouldn't work. He said he was going to tell Anna. I couldn't let that happen. I was stringing her along so she wouldn't suspect me, hinting that I'd run off to Poland with her. If Tomek told her, it would all be over."

"So you killed Tomek?" Claire stepped back. "And framed it as suicide?"

"I thought it was convincing." He winced, half keeling over. "I dumped the gun in the forest knowing his prints would be all over it and nicked the rope from a narrowboat. I thought they'd put two and two together and call it a closed case, although I didn't expect it to take them so long to find him hanging there. Who knew they could tell the difference between kinds of strangling?"

In the square, several sets of tyres screeched.

"Dad," Leo said, approaching for the first time. "You said you had nothing to do with Tomek's death. You promised."

"Oh, son." Duncan inhaled, wheezing like he had lungs full of rusty nails. "What does it matter? You couldn't go to the police either way. You're involved. Both of you are. If you go to the police about any of this, the gang will kill you. Look what they did to me. They only let me live on the off chance they could get their crap on the shelves again."

She heard her name, first from Damon and then Ryan.

"You're a monster," Leo whispered.

"I got you this job, didn't I?" Duncan stared at Leo from beneath lowered brows, hands clutching his middle. "I dropped hints to Anna about updating Eryk's life insurance in case anything went wrong, didn't I? I only did what needed to be done. Your problem, Leo, is you're just too nice."

Duncan doubled over, and Claire thought he'd passed out, but he'd used the distraction to reach under the inflatable bed and pull out a shotgun.

"And you," he said, pointing it at Claire. "You're

exactly like Eryk's descriptions of your mother. A chip off the old nosey, know-it-all block." He nodded at the gun. "What? Did you think they sent me back unable to defend myself? They might have locked me up and almost beat me to death, but I'm still of use to them as long as this post office is mine. Not like I can pay them what I owe from prison, is it? We're all in too deep to turn back now."

"Dad..."

"Are you going to keep your mouth shut, Claire?" Duncan asked, taking a step towards her. "Or do I need to silence you like I did Tomek?"

The hollow barrels of the shotgun stared at her like eyeless sockets. Her father's voice in her head told her to remain calm, not to run, and to go along with what the madman was saying. She swapped the barrels for Duncan, but his stare was just as hollow. Just as deadly. It was already too late to run.

But she wasn't going to lie.

"You're a murderer," she said. "You'll pay for what you did."

"No." Duncan shook his head, taking another menacing step forward. "The only person who is going to pay is–"

Leo tackled Duncan onto the bed, and Claire ducked as the gun fired and blew a hole through the ceiling above her. She jumped back; as the dust cleared, the blue sky and birds were visible above her. In the square, chaos unfolded yet again.

Leo slid the gun across the floor and out of reach. He pinned Duncan to the bed, not that he needed much restraining. The tackle had knocked out the wind that had been holding his battered body upright, along with the inflatable bed. It hissed and slowly started to sink to the floorboards.

Duncan coughed mouthfuls of blood onto the white sheets, eyes clenched tight. Claire pulled Leo off him, but Duncan didn't try to rise.

"Call him an ambulance," Claire said, resting a hand on Leo's shoulder. "It's over."

Leo glared at his coughing father as he scrambled for his phone. While Leo dialled the number, Duncan crawled forward, reaching for the gun though it was metres away. He was in no fit state to even stand, but Claire picked up the shotgun anyway; she wasn't taking another chance.

The gun was heavier than she'd expected.

She pointed it at Duncan, but she couldn't even pretend she was anything like him. She lowered it as he flopped backwards as the bed's firmness vanished, just as poor Eryk had done on the pavement outside exactly a week earlier.

Even after everything he'd done – perhaps because of everything he'd done – she hoped he'd live to face justice. Death was too easy an option for someone who had murdered a father and son to cover his own slimy tracks.

"Thank you," she said to Leo when he got off the phone. "I think you might have just saved my life."

Having heard everything she needed to hear, she passed Leo the gun and left after the paramedics rushed up the stairs.

Afternoon sunlight pushed through the gaps in the chipboard that had replaced the glass in the dark and empty post office. She would have preferred a random burglary over the truth, even if it meant her instincts had been wrong.

"Claire!" her father rushed down the back alley, using the wall for support in lieu of his cane. "Thank goodness! I thought they'd got you. The cars sped off and then it sounded like another gunshot. I thought … I thought …"

"I was in the post office," she said, glancing at the curtain over the rear window. "Well, the flat above it. It's over."

"I know," he said, reaching her. "They got the go ahead. They're arresting everyone as we speak. It's done." Alan searched her face. "Wait, why were you in the post office?"

"I'll tell you over a coffee," she said as they headed back to her shop. "You might want to call the station. If they can spare any officers, they'll want to hear this too."

CHAPTER SEVENTEEN

*O*ne week later, on Claire's thirty-sixth birthday, she was more than happy to be alone in her closed candle shop after another busy Saturday. She placed the final shiny jar, completing the circular display of identical white candles.

Perfecting the new and improved fresh linen scent had taken a while, but she'd nailed it with the fifth version. A hint more Egyptian musk and a dash less jasmine had been all it needed. Simple when she knew the answer, but much like Eryk and Tomek's murders, she had to go around the houses to get there.

After kicking the cardboard box through to the back room, she flicked off the lights and headed upstairs. The flat had been relatively tidy when she'd left that morning, but now it glimmered like a show home.

"You cleaned up."

"I couldn't help myself," Janet said, lying on Claire's bed and flicking through the latest issue of the *Northash Observer*. A fresh linen candle glimmered on the bedside table. "And before you ask why I'm rereading the article, it's because I'm very proud of you."

"Better than the women's magazines," she said. "They'd never have gone with 'Business Owner Busts Bargain Booze Murder Madness!' for a headline."

"And a *hair* more interesting," she said, tracing the words with a finger. "'When asked where her unlikely detective skills came from, candle shop owner, Claire Harris, credited her father, Detective Inspector Alan Harris, now retired.' He cried when he saw that."

"It's only the truth." She settled on the bed. "Though 'detective skills' is a push."

Janet slapped the paper shut and picked up her compact mirror to put in her diamond studs. Claire had been happy to oblige when her mother had asked if she could get ready for their drinks at the pub away from Moreen's watchful eye.

"This new candle might be your best yet." Janet

inhaled as she fastened the stud at the back. "If you ever stop making this one, we'll be having words."

Claire grinned, pleased by how much her mother loved it. She'd made the candle specifically for her, after all – though she'd kept that part to herself.

"Don't worry, it's here to stay." She dragged her finger around the front-page picture of Duncan, in a wheelchair, being escorted out of the hospital by police. "Tonight's only a few drinks at the pub, isn't it? No surprise party?"

"No party." Janet blinked into a mascara wand. "That's what you asked for." She dunked the wand again. "You'll never guess who I saw this morning."

A quick change of subject was never a good sign.

"Who?" she asked, playing along.

"Linda and Joan from the WI." Janet closed the mascara and tossed it into her small makeup bag. "Barred from the shop, eh?"

"I can explain."

"You don't need to." She grabbed Claire's hand. "Even though they denied saying anything bad about me, I know you wouldn't have blown up like that unless you had a reason. I never liked them much anyway, so thank you."

"You feeling alright, Mum?"

"I am." She inhaled, rubbing the back of Claire's

hand with her thumb. "I'm feeling grateful that, for whatever reason, you're always fighting in my corner. I haven't always been the best to you, Claire."

"Oh, give over." Claire shuffled next to her mum and hugged her. "The past is the past. I love where our relationship is right now."

Janet's face lit up.

"Really?"

"Really." Claire kissed her mum on the cheek. "Just promise if you ever commit light fraud again you won't keep it such a secret."

"I promise."

In the chaos of Eryk's shooting, Tomek's hanging, the allotment raid, and Duncan's confession, Janet's pension fraud had, thankfully, slipped through the cracks. A cheque to the council to make up the money seemed to be enough.

"And try to bottle things up a little less," said Claire firmly. "Emotions aren't ugly, despite what your mother tells you. You don't have to be fine all the time. And even if you don't want to let all the Joans and Lindas know, don't hide the bad stuff from your family. You can tell me anything."

"Anything?" Janet inhaled. "I'm terrified of the future. I don't know what to do with myself now. The post office was all I've ever known. Forty years. I feel like I'm being put out to pasture, but I'm not ready to retire."

"Then don't."

"But I'm not good at anything," she said, sighing. "Not really. Who would hire me?"

"Now you're just being silly." Claire headed to the wardrobe to find something to wear. "You're brilliant, Mum. You file my accounts, you can organise like nobody's business, and look at what you did to my flat in half an hour. It looks like nobody even lives here, it's that clean. You have more transferable skills than most people in the job market."

"But what do I *do*?"

"Who says you need to figure it out right now?" Claire pulled two hangers from the wardrobe and showed them to her mum. "Which one?"

Janet assessed both, and Claire almost regretted asking. Her mother never agreed with her fashion choices, safe as they usually were. Anything that hadn't originated in Marks and Spencer's clothing department didn't typically live up to her mother's formal, middle-class standards.

"Which do you like?" Janet asked instead.

Claire almost made a sarcastic comment about needing to check her mother's temperature, but she refrained. She'd felt several shifts since the night Eryk dropped his bombshell on Janet in the sitting room. Not all had been good, but since Duncan's arrest, Janet's attitude seemed to have shifted once more. Maybe it was only a couple of degrees to the left, but it was a change, nonetheless.

Claire opted for a scoop-necked black blouse, dark grey fitted jeans, and an oversized cream blazer. In the mirror, she looked altogether more grown-up than usual … but, then, her mother wasn't the only one who had shifted.

Before her last birthday, she'd been single, living with her parents, and working in a factory. She barely recognised that life. And she loved the one she was living now.

Claire waited at the top of the stairs while her mother ran the taps in the bathroom. The gushing water wasn't loud enough to cover the whispering.

"Ready?" Janet asked as she walked out.

"Let's go."

As she'd suspected, she heard a round of shushing as they approached the unusually quiet pub across the square. A chorus of "Surprise!" hit her like a wave as she entered the packed pub, where every face she knew from around the village was present and accounted for.

Last year, the idea of a surprise party in her honour

would have made her skin crawl, but amazingly, she only felt love as the grinning faces crowded around her.

"Do you hate me?" Ryan whispered into her ear as he hugged her. "I've missed so many birthdays, I couldn't resist."

"So much for a quiet drink," she said before kissing him. "But I could never hate you. How long have you been planning this?"

"He's been at it all month." Sally gave her a sideways hug. "Why do you think we all kept asking what you were doing for your birthday?"

"I had noticed. Cheers for giving me the heads up, mate."

"Wouldn't have been a surprise."

"Enough chat!" Damon clapped his hands. "It's a crime that the birthday girl doesn't already have a pint of homebrew in her hand."

While Theresa pulled Claire the traditional free birthday pint, she scanned the pub. Em and Ash were chatting in a quiet corner, and for the first time, Claire witnessed Ash's smile.

"Your mother managed to get in touch with his father," Alan whispered to Claire as he joined her at the bar. "He seemed shocked to hear how Ash was living."

"Didn't he kick him out?"

"He did," he said with a nod, "but it seemed like he wanted to make amends. He's supposed to be showing his face here to talk things through. For the child's sake, let's hope he does."

Another absent father and another of her birthday parties; Claire hoped history didn't repeat itself.

When she depleted her first pint, Damon placed another directly in her hand. She had a feeling it was going to be one of those nights where she didn't have to put her hand in her pocket. And if it were, tomorrow would be one of those mornings she'd be glad she didn't have to open the shop.

An hour into the party, while Ryan and Claire fought in doubles against Damon and Sally at the pool table, Leo popped his head through the door. She passed her pint to Sally and joined him in the small vestibule.

"Happy birthday," he said, handing her a yellow envelope. "Hope you don't mind if I don't join in. I'm not sure I can face people yet."

"Not at all," she said. "You're looking well."

"I am?" He pushed up his glasses. "Thanks. It feels good to be sleeping again. Most nights, anyway. The police dropping the charges against me has helped. My dad gave a statement saying I was coerced."

"You say that like he did you a favour. You *were* coerced."

"I know." He peered down at his shoes. "No matter how scared I was, I still had a choice, and I did make things worse. Berna keeps reminding me the situation was bigger than me. Maybe she's right."

"You were just a guy working in the wrong place at the wrong time." She patted his shoulder. "How's Berna doing?"

"As good as can be expected, given the circumstances," he said, pushing his hands into his pockets. "Anna too. They're settling in with Anna's sister. Being around their family seems to be helping."

"Funny how that usually does the trick."

"Yeah," he said sadly. "I ... I don't really have anyone left now."

"Oh, Leo, I'm sorry. I didn't mean it like that."

"No, it's fine." He smiled. "Listen, I'm not just here to give you that card. I'm here to say goodbye too."

"Where are you going?"

"Poland," he said, exhaling heavily. "Berna's asked me to fly over. We're going to see how things go. After everything my dad did, I never thought she'd give me another chance."

They stepped aside to let a short man with dark blond hair walk past them and into the pub.

"Is that what you want to do?"

"I have nothing left here," he said, looking over his shoulder into the darkening square. "Don't even have a job now. I have no idea what it'll be like living in Poland, but I'll be with the girl I love. And I'll be there for our baby. Growing up, my dad wasn't really there for me. After my mum died, he stepped up a little bit, but look how that turned out."

Claire hadn't known Leo's mother was dead. She knew little about him other than he was the young guy in the post office with the glasses and mild acne who'd get endearingly flustered whenever she went in.

"I suppose I should go and pack," he said, tensing up his shoulders as he rocked back on his heels. "Ticket is booked for the morning. Don't suppose you know which buses get near the airport?"

"I usually get a taxi."

"Ah, I can't afford that." He rocked again. "For all Eryk's faults, he always paid me on time. That wasn't so much a priority for the week my dad was in charge."

Claire pulled her purse from her blazer pocket, fished out all the notes she had, and stuffed them into Leo's hands. It was at least a hundred pounds. She definitely couldn't have made the gesture on her last birthday; it was another potent reminder of just how far she'd come in a year.

"Claire, I can't—"

"It's my birthday," she said, putting her purse away. "I'm about to get very drunk for free, so it's not up for discussion. It's only what I would have spent buying rounds. Why don't you come in for one? Nobody will say anything."

"I'm not sure."

"It's your last night in Northash," she said, wrapping her arm around his shoulders. "You can't leave without one last pint of Hesketh Homebrew."

Once she had Leo set up at the bar with her father, DI Ramsbottom drifted over with a plate from the buffet.

"You came across well on the news," she said, lifting her drink to him, an unspoken 'well, this time', lingering in her pause. "Enjoy your moment of glory?"

"Much better without a *pesky* journalist trying to catch me out." He bit into a cocktail sausage. "It's your name on the front page, though, not that you don't deserve it."

"You'll get the next one," said Alan. "Join me for a whisky."

As Ramsbottom climbed onto a tiny barstool, she looked over to the corner. Ash was sitting with the man who had snuck in through the vestibule. They were locked in a tight embrace, both crying.

"It's not natural, is it?" hissed Moreen, standing by the bar and sipping her plain tomato juice. "A boy with hair that long. Looks like a girl, and you know how I feel about that. It's not right."

"Oh, Mother," Janet snapped. "Give it a rest."

"Don't backchat, girl!"

For a split second, Claire thought her mother would apologise and go back to her wine. Instead, Janet put down the glass and rose from her bar stool.

"Why does it matter how long Ash's hair is?" Janet asked, her eyes firmly on her mother. "Well?"

"It's not normal."

"Why?" Janet pushed. "What difference does it make to you? What difference does anything that anyone does make to you?"

Moreen stiffened, nostrils flaring. "Watch your tongue, Janet. You forget to whom you are speaking."

"Oh, I know exactly who I'm talking to."

"I am your *mother*!"

"I am your daughter." Janet planted her hands on her hips. "And I've had enough of your poison. *Enough*. When does it stop? When do you realise that the things you say can hurt people?"

"Like you're a saint."

Moreen's voice rose so loudly the chatter died down around the bar. Theresa and Malcolm trained

242

their eyes on mother and daughter, clearly ready to jump in when needed.

"You're right." Janet tossed her hands out. "I'm not innocent. I'm more like you than I want to be. The way you brought me up to fear you, the control – I don't want that. You infected me."

"This is how you speak to your mother?" Moreen slammed her glass down on the bar, spilling tomato juice. "No wonder your daughter's such a perpetual disappointment."

Gasps shuddered through the silence, but Claire only shrugged. No matter the subject, Moreen always got her digs in whenever she could.

"Despite me, my daughter turned out wonderfully," Janet said, holding her head high even as her bottom lip quivered. "You're nothing but a bully, Mother."

"A *bully*?" Moreen stretched out a finger. "You know nothing. Had I ever spoken to my mother as you're speaking to me now, she would already have lashed me with the cane. At least I never hit you!"

"So, that's how you sleep at night?"

More gasps followed, but Claire was too stunned to react. For the first time in her life, Moreen looked speechless. Her mouth gaped as she tried to say something, but the words didn't come.

"Why are you still in Northash if you hate it so

much?" Janet asked.

"I wanted to spend time with my family."

"Then you have a funny way of showing it." Janet exhaled and looked down for the first time. "I'm too old and too tired to put up with you anymore, Mother. If you want to spend your final days spitting acid, go right ahead. I choose not to be around it. I need to break this cycle. I think the time has come for you to go home."

Behind her snarl, Moreen looked as though she was fighting back tears. But she'd never let them fall, not even when faced with her daughter's honesty.

"Very well," she said, primly clasping her hands at her waist. "I will be on the first train home in the morning."

Moreen turned on her heel and left, though the mood in the pub didn't immediately revert to what it had been.

Janet collapsed onto her stool and picked up her wine as Alan clutched her free hand.

"Good for you," Greta said, patting her on the back. "Good for you, Janet."

"Was I too harsh?"

"I'd say you were positively restrained, dear," Alan said, raising his glass. "You didn't say anything that wasn't true."

"She's ninety."

"Which just means she's old enough to know better," Greta said before clapping her hands several times. "Right, everyone, you've had your performance for the evening. Back to it. My definitely *not* disappointing Claire's birthday isn't going to celebrate itself."

As the party reluctantly picked up, Claire hugged her mother from behind.

"I'm sorry for doing that tonight of all nights. I should have waited."

"No, you shouldn't." Claire squeezed tight. "I'm proud of you, Mum."

It took another round of drinks and Theresa turning up the music for the party atmosphere to return. Ryan and Claire beat Sally and Damon at pool three times in a row before they gave up and stopped asking for rematches.

"I probably should have mentioned I got quite good at pool in Spain," Ryan whispered to Claire as Sally and Damon wandered off. "Is something going on with those two?"

"Oh, absolutely," she whispered back as they slunk off through the front door one after the other. "I don't know what, exactly, but it's sweet they think I haven't noticed."

"I would never have put them together," he said, wrapping his arm around her shoulders, "but it kind of works."

"Apparently they have *chemistry*." Claire chuckled as she took the first sip of her third pint. "Not that Sally admitted who she was talking about, but I know."

In the corner, Ash and his father stood after almost an hour of deep conversation. As they walked to the door, Janet followed them out.

"Glad to see his dad showed up," Ryan said, pulling away to line up the pool balls for another game. "Do you remember your fourteenth birthday party?"

"I do," she said. "Do you remember my hat?"

"The hat." Ryan laughed. "The *haircut*."

"And your dad."

"You remember?"

"Of course." She passed him his pool cue. "Maybe if I'd remembered earlier, I would have understood your point of view about the card. You were right. I didn't get it."

"No." Ryan rubbed chalk on the cue. "*You* were right. I showed Amelia, and we had a very long, honest talk about how it might just be a card and nothing more. It wasn't easy, but being a single dad doesn't come with a guidebook."

"You're doing a better job than most," Claire said.

Ryan sent the white ball hurtling to the triangle of red and yellow. The balls scattered, immediately potting a yellow. "Maybe it's my old age, but I don't remember you mentioning your dad after that."

"I didn't." He passed the cue to Claire and helped her line it up on the corner. "When he didn't show up, I called and told him to leave me alone. I didn't want any more disappointment. I expected him to apologise, but he just said 'Okay', and that was that."

"Oh, Ryan."

"I've had years to get over it." He finished lining up her shot. "Go on. Give it some welly."

Claire struck the white ball, though the red ball he'd lined her up to pocket missed by an inch and rolled back to the middle.

Instead of pushing the topic further, they continued their game of pool. Claire could tell Ryan was holding back, but she still lost.

"I just saw Sally and Damon snogging by the clock!" Janet cried when she returned. "I thought I was seeing things."

"As long as they're having fun." Claire laughed before realising her mother was alone. "Where's Ash?"

"He's gone home with his father," she said with a tight smile. "I spoke with Justin on the phone for hours last night. I didn't expect it, but I had him sobbing by the end of the call. Somehow, he didn't realise how much pain rejecting his child had caused until I spelt it out for him."

"Do you think they'll be okay?"

"I really hope so," she said, glancing at the door. "I grew fond of Ash. He brought out my soft side, I think. I'll be checking in every day to make sure they're on the right track. One whiff of trouble, and Justin will have me to answer to."

"If that doesn't scare him, nothing will."

"Very funny." Janet winked. "By the way, I've had a thought about my future. It might be the drama of the evening or the wine talking, but it doesn't seem like such a bad idea."

"Go on."

"I think I might start my own business," she whispered, glancing around the pub. "If you can do it, why can't I? I think I'd be quite good at it."

"Are you kidding?" Claire laughed. "You could send an army into battle and win. Of course you'd be good at it. What kind of business?"

"A cleaning business," she said, gazing off into the middle distance. "I can see it now. A fleet of employees cleaning the length and breadth of Lancashire. Perhaps even the whole country!"

Claire arched an amused brow. "Maybe start with Northash?"

"Janet's Angels, bringing sparkle and shine one home at a time." She squinted into the corner of the room as though seeing something nobody else could. "Anyway, I'll leave you to it. Nature calls."

"Oh, and me." Claire took another gulp of her drink. "Watch that, Ryan."

After a quick bathroom break where they discussed the business idea more thoroughly through the stall walls, Claire returned to find her pint and Ryan gone. As she looked around for him, Em caught her eye.

"He's out back," she said with a badly suppressed smile. "He's waiting for you."

Unsure if she could handle any more surprises tonight, Claire headed into the beer garden. The twinkling fairy lights beat back the darkness with their warm glow.

Ryan leaned against the railing beside the canal, staring at the dark forest. As Claire approached, she noticed he was holding a rectangular shape wrapped in brown paper.

"Should we go on a narrowboat trip?" he asked when Claire leaned against the railing beside him. "Em keeps suggesting it."

"Ask me when I don't have a belly full of beer." Her stomach turned at the very thought. "That for me?"

"It is." He sucked air through his teeth as he handed over the package, and the shadows of the night didn't hide how flushed his cheeks were. "Didn't want to give it to you with everyone around."

Claire ripped back the paper to reveal the back of a frame. She turned it over to see the image of them together on the stairs from her sixteenth birthday, only this time in delicate watercolours.

"I don't know what to say." She blinked back her tears. "It's beautiful. You've outdone yourself."

"Thanks." His blush deepened. "Do you remember that party?"

"Too well."

"Doesn't seem like twenty years ago."

"No," she said, looking out at the water. "And yes. Does that make sense?"

"Absolutely." He chuckled. "Do you want to know something funny about that party? I almost asked you to be my girlfriend."

Claire almost dropped the frame into the canal as her heart skipped several beats.

"R-really?" she stammered, barely able to feign casualness. "I never knew that."

"Sally said something to me," he explained, slow

laughing. "She said 'Don't you think you and Claire would make a great couple?' after I'd had a can of cider. I hadn't thought about it before, but I reckoned she might be right. I was all set to ask you, but I chickened out when I saw you."

"That's funny." Claire could hardly look at him. "Weird."

"Yeah."

As the party roared behind them, they gazed out at the water together. In the silence, what if scenarios swirled in Claire's mind.

"Claire?"

"Yeah?"

"Do you want to be my girlfriend?" he said. "I just realised I hadn't asked."

Claire ducked her head and laughed.

"That reaction is the reason I didn't ask twenty years ago."

"No, it's not that," she said, still laughing. "I already thought I was."

Safe in their little bubble of calm by the railing, they kissed. Behind them, the party grew louder and louder. Finally, the back door burst open, and they reluctantly pulled apart.

"C'mon, you two!" Sally cried from the front of a conga line, with Damon behind her. "Join on the back!

We're doing a lap of the square."

As the conga line passed, Claire joined Granny Greta, and Ryan held on to her. They danced down the side path to the square until they couldn't even hear the pub's music – only their laughter and chanting as they kicked out their legs.

She didn't know if it was her birthday, the homebrew, or Ryan's arms around her waist, but her chest swelled with warmth.

Claire no longer loved Ryan the way she'd done as a teenager; she loved him more.

And for the first time in her life, she let herself believe Ryan might feel the same way.

I hope you enjoyed another trip to Northash! If you did, **DON'T FORGET TO RATE AND REVIEW ON AMAZON!**

The 6th book in the Claire's Candles series, TOFFEE APPLE TORMENT, is coming AUGUST 31st 2021! PRE-ORDER now!

WANT TO BE KEPT UP TO DATE WITH AGATHA
FROST RELEASES? *SIGN UP THE FREE
NEWSLETTER!*

www.AgathaFrost.com

You can also follow **Agatha Frost** across social media.
Search 'Agatha Frost' on:

Facebook
Twitter
Goodreads
Instagram

Claire's Candles

1. Vanilla Bean Vengeance

2. Black Cherry Betrayal

3. Coconut Milk Casualty

4. Rose Petal Revenge

5. Fresh Linen Fraud (NEW!)

6. Toffee Apple Torment (PRE-ORDER!)

Peridale Cafe

1. Pancakes and Corpses

2. Lemonade and Lies

3. Doughnuts and Deception

4. Chocolate Cake and Chaos

5. Shortbread and Sorrow

6. Espresso and Evil

7. Macarons and Mayhem

8. Fruit Cake and Fear

9. Birthday Cake and Bodies

10. Gingerbread and Ghosts

Other